Chika U

Night Dancer

JONATHAN CAPE
LONDON

Published by Jonathan Cape 2012

2 4 6 8 10 9 7 5 3 1

Copyright © Chika Unigwe 2012

Chika Unigwe has asserted her right under the Copyright, Designs
and Patents Act 1988 to be identified as the author of this work

This book is sold subject to the condition that it shall not, by way of trade or
otherwise, be lent, resold, hired out, or otherwise circulated without the
publisher's prior consent in any form of binding or cover other than that
in which it is published and without a similar condition, including
this condition, being imposed on the subsequent purchaser

First published in Great Britain in 2012 by
Jonathan Cape
Random House, 20 Vauxhall Bridge Road,
London SW1V 2SA

www.vintage-books.co.uk

Addresses for companies within The Random House Group Limited
can be found at: www.randomhouse.co.uk/offices.htm

The Random House Group Limited Reg. No. 954009

A CIP catalogue record for this book
is available from the British Library

ISBN 9780224093835

The Random House Group Limited supports The Forest Stewardship Council
(FSC®), the leading international forest certification organisation. Our books
carrying the FSC label are printed on FSC® certified paper. FSC is the only forest
certification scheme endorsed by the leading environmental organisations, including
Greenpeace. Our paper procurement policy can be found at
www.randomhouse.co.uk/environment

MIX
Paper from
responsible sources
FSC® C016897

Typeset in Bembo by Palimpsest Book Production Limited
Falkirk, Stirlingshire
Printed and bound in Great Britain by
Clays Ltd, St Ives Plc

With love for my people

Part 1

Onwu egbuchughi ji e jiri chu aja, e mesie o pue ome.

If the yam used in sacrifice does not die prematurely,
it will eventually germinate.

Igbo proverb

Enugu, 2001

1

On the third day, she went back to see Madam Gold. 'The problem is that those with buttocks do not know how to sit!' Madam Gold declared firmly. 'That was your mother's problem.' She shifted in her half of the settee as if the reference to buttocks had made her suddenly self-conscious of her own.

'Ah, may this heat not kill us, oo,' she said, pulling off her bobbed wig to reveal sparse greying hair held untidily by a rubber band at the top of her head. 'I don't know how you can bear to have such heavy braids in this heat, Mma.'

Mma smiled back in response.

Madam Gold reached one massive, wobbly hand into her bra, pulled out a flower-patterned handkerchief and wiped the sweat off her face. She tucked the handkerchief back in, turned to Mma, and in one swift movement, flung her arms around her. She whispered fiercely, 'I know what life is like for a young girl like you.'

Both the remark and the hug took Mma by surprise. Madam Gold, her mother's best friend, was not given to displays of affection. She released Mma as suddenly as she had grabbed her, as if she herself was surprised by the hug, and said almost tenderly, 'Your mother was stubborn. Very stubborn.' She moved her hands over

Mma's face. 'Every man deserves a son.' She paused. She looked like she was weighing her words, trying them out in her head before releasing them.

'Every man . . . a man like . . . Your father was . . . a man . . . Especially a man who had been as patient as your father was. Your father was very patient. Yes. Not even a man carved out of stone would turn away a son when his wife had only been able to give him a daughter.' Her voice rose: 'I'm not saying that what he did was right. *Mba nu!* I'm only saying that he did what any man in his position would have done. Any man, *nwoke obuna*, would have done the same. Would have looked elsewhere. It's only natural. They would have planted their seeds in many places, hoping that at least one would sprout. Anybody who tells you otherwise is lying. Are you listening to me? *I na-egekwa m nti?*'

'Yes, Aunty.' She was grateful when Madam Gold released her face. She had held her breath through the speech, for the older woman stank as if she had just eaten beans. Or boiled eggs. She'd had to resist the urge to pull her head back from the assault.

Madam Gold picked up the glass of water from the side table beside her and began to drink. For a long time the gurgling noise was the only sound in the room. *Glup. Glup. Glup.* 'This heat keeps my throat dry all day,' she said. She craned her neck behind her and shouted into the kitchen for more water. Her maid, a little girl of about eight, came scrambling out with a plastic jar and placed it on the table. But she did not go away. She stood there, a sheet of paper in her hand, half held out to Madam Gold.

6

'*Ogini*? What is that, *Ebele*?' Madam Gold asked impatiently.

'It's a list, Ma. For supper. I need to go to the market before it closes.'

Madam Gold took the list from her and scanned it.

'Didn't you buy Maggi cubes yesterday?'

'Yes, Ma, but we used them all up in stew last night.'

Madam Gold hissed. She dragged a brown handbag from under the settee and counted out some notes. She gave the money to the girl and dismissed her with a 'Don't waste time there, oo. Just buy what you need to buy and come home straight!' She replaced her bag, looked at Mma and said, 'You know, when we were younger, our parents could buy food in bulk to keep at home, not like these days when you have to rush out each time you need to cook to buy onion and Maggi cubes! Who can afford to buy anything in bulk these days, eh?'

Mma sat on the edge of the settee, her hands clenched in her laps, saying nothing. She was not really listening to Madam Gold any more. She wondered what it was she felt. Her throat was parched but she had not asked for a drink when she came in and now she could not. She would just have to bear it.

So, she had a brother somewhere. She could have had a 'happy-happy' family, the sort of normal family her mother had mocked in her usual way: 'All those happy-happy families you see everywhere, scratch them, lift the lid and all you'll see are many sad-sad things, dirty-dirty things.'

Every child deserved a father. Indeed. Especially a child with a mother like hers to balance out her life.

7

Whatever hurt this father might have caused could not be that bad, if Madam Gold, sensible Madam Gold, had said that any man would have done what he did. He had not sent her mother packing; she had walked out. Whatever had happened she, not he, must be blamed for the consequences. Her mother had no right to keep her away from him, or him away from her. It was not right. If only she had been allowed contact, her life would have turned out differently. She would have talked about him at school. She could have stood in front of the class, all proud, and said, 'My father is an architect.' Or, 'My father is a painter.' What did he do? She had no idea. She could ask Madam Gold. He was a real person.

'What does . . . what did he do, Aunty? My father?' It was difficult knowing whether to speak about him in the present or the past. What if he was dead? She chided herself for even thinking it. She would not permit such thoughts. Not now.

'Business. He was a businessman. I suppose he's still a businessman.'

'What sort?'

'He had a supermarket. One of the best in Kaduna then. Sold everything. Anything you couldn't find, you couldn't find anywhere else. Such was its reputation. Your mother used to complain that he kept her awake at night talking about his plans for his business, simulating change on a sheet of paper, drawing and erasing where items ought to be placed for maximum sales. Every few months he moved stock around, said it kept customers interested.'

Her father was a successful businessman. Someone she

could have been proud of. The sort of man any young man would have been happy to introduce as his father-in-law. If he had been in her life she would not have had boyfriends date her and then dump her for a more suitable candidate. Or have Obi drag his feet about her now. She would make any man a good wife, one ex-boyfriend had told her, 'it is just your mother. And we're not *oyibo*, oo, we are not white people, for whom love is enough.' (He had married someone more suitable soon afterwards.) He was right. Everyone knew that marriage here was not an intimate affair between two people like it was with the *oyibos*.

Madam Gold poured some more water into her glass from the white plastic jar, and said loudly, as if she was angry, 'Your mother could have stayed. She should have stayed. What else could your father have done? What could he have done? Your mother was stubborn. I talked and talked to her, but my words went into one ear and straight out through the other. Her mind was made up. When you give medicine to a very sick man and his penis rises up, it is best to leave him alone as he has already found a woman on the other side. Nothing could change your mother's mind.'

She paused as if exhausted. 'Your father loved your mother, which is more than many wives have. He loved her. She knew that and I think she wanted to punish him by taking away what would hurt him the most. The problem was that she loved him too. She forgot that it never makes sense to cut off your own nose to spite your face. Everything, everything she had worked for, she gave up the moment she walked out. And for what? For that slip of a girl. A mere girl! She was not even

9

beautiful, that Rapu.' She shook her head slowly from side to side, like a masquerade performer worn out from a day of running and dancing in the heat. 'I know my place. And I know what the options are outside these four walls. What do you think I'd do if my husband took another wife tomorrow? We women are little people. Your mother forgot that. I'm not condoning what Rapu did. I am not condoning what your father did, God forbid. I was upset when I heard. I mean, I could hardly believe that Mike would do such a thing. We always thought he was different. But I told Ezi, "What's done is done."'

She let out a hollow, unexpected laugh. 'Your mother was brave to take the steps she did, to walk out without looking back. Not even once. She shut that door and she never went back. That has to take quite some guts. E was fearless. Me, I am not brave enough. But I also know that there is wisdom sometimes in not being brave. You can only fight while you are alive. What is it they say in English? "You *leev* to fight another day." I told her that. She was my best friend and it was my duty to tell her the truth. But she would not listen to anyone. Once your mother's mind was made up, there was no changing it. You know that; you grew up with her, you know how she could be.'

She exhaled loudly, as if she had been holding her breath. 'Women cannot afford that kind of stubbornness. Are you listening to me? *I na-egekwa m nti*, Adamma?'

'Yes.' There were not many people who called her by her full name. Her mother had screamed it at her when she was really angry. 'Adamma, come and pick up the schoolbag you've left lying around here!'

'There is no place for that kind of stubbornness in a woman's life. Are you listening to me?'

'Yes, Aunty.'

'Good. But your mother was meant to be a man. Ah, my dear friend . . .' She smiled and shook her head gently. 'Your mother would have made a good man. She came in the wrong body. That's all.' She sighed again.

Afraid of being surprised by another hug, Mma bent down and started to scratch an imaginary itch on her leg. Her skin turned chalky white and she remembered that she had come out without rubbing on any lotion. She had skin which needed constant moisturising in the harmattan, even if the harmattan was as freakishly hot as this year's. She tried to rub the whiteness off with her thumb without much success. She also noticed that in her haste she had put on the rubber slippers she normally only ever wore at home. She hadn't worn rubber slippers outside since she was fifteen. And their purple colour did not go at all with her light green dress.

A reflective silence surrounded them for a short while. Madam Gold looked at her. 'Rapu was nowhere near your mother. That girl was nowhere near E at all! No comparison. She was flat both front and back. Teeth like a rabbit. No buttocks, no breasts. As skinny as a chewing stick.' She exhaled again. 'Yet . . . men will sleep with anything.'

Mma tried to imagine Rapu, skinny as a chewing stick with teeth like a rabbit's. Her mother, although not as big as Madam Gold, had body. She was full without being fat. Maybe Rapu had had the waif-like look of a supermodel. She wanted to tell Madam Gold, 'Aunty, my mother did not come in the wrong body, and she was not brave. She was selfish.' But once she thought of that, she remembered all the other things she had discovered about her mother: things that were making her look at her in another light, in another way, as if she were discovering a total stranger. The remembrance brought a smell to her nose: the smell of something she would rather forget. The smell of something white. The smell of her upside-down thoughts. She could no longer stay.

G is for guilt. And for go. 'One of the most useful lessons life has taught me,' her mother had written, 'is knowing when to get up and go. There is nothing as resented as the guest who has outstayed his welcome.' The guilt was new for Mma, precipitated by the discoveries she was making about her mother, through the letters she had left behind.

Mma got up. 'I should be leaving, Aunty. Thank you.' A bottle of Fanta had been brought out. She had not even noticed.

'Wait,' Madam Gold said. 'I have something to give you.'

2

On the second day after she began to read the letters, Mma could think of nowehere to go but to Madam Gold's. Her mother had left her a trove of stories. Memoirs, Mma corrected herself, sticking to her mother's description. Half-told stories. Unformed stories she had to birth, midwifed by Madam Gold. Her mother called Madam Gold G. Madam Gold, on her part, called Mma's mother E. Just the initials, in the intimate short-hand of best friends and confidantes. Mma knew that if anyone could fill in the gaps in her mother's story, it would be Madam Gold.

She told Madam Gold about how, intending to go to bed, she had found herself instead walking to her mother's room, lantern in hand, as there had been a power cut.

'I didn't even think I was going to go there!'

Madam Gold said, 'Man proposes, God disposes. It isn't inexplicable. Your mother's spirit dragged you in. She wanted you to read her story.'

'She's dead, Aunty!'

'And the dead live among us. The line between us and them is just a breath away.'

'Maybe,' Mma said, shrugging her shoulders. She did not want to think of her mother guiding her movements from beyond the grave. The thought was depressing. She did not tell Madam Gold that the moment she turned the handle of her mother's door, the power was restored, as if both actions were linked. She had almost dropped the lantern from the shock of it. She did not want Madam Gold telling her that her mother had something to do with that as well. She had always thought she was too modern, too intelligent, to believe in the dead having powers or feelings, but now she was not so sure. No. In fact, now she rather hoped that they did. After all, what was the point of her seeking revenge if her mother was oblivious to it? If she could not ensure that her mother's spirit never rested?

'How could you have had the letters for this long but never bothered to read them?' Madam Gold asked.

Mma shrugged.

'You're just your mother's daughter.'

Mma shook her head by way of response. What could she tell Madam Gold? That she wanted so much to be rid of her mother that she had not wanted to read the letters? That she was afraid that the letters might reveal something that would call into question all her righteous indignation at the dead woman? She did not believe Madam Gold's thesis that her mother's spirit had somehow engineered it. But something had happened to cause her change of heart. She had not even been curious, certain that she knew as much about her mother as she cared to know. It was probably, she thought, a combination of things: a dream she had been trying to forget, the power cut, boredom. There had been nothing to distract her. She knew better than to tell Madam Gold this. She would just try to convince Mma that responsibility for her change of mind lay with the dead woman.

'I wasn't ever going to read the letters, Aunty. That night, I was just going to go to my room and sleep. Even when I got to my mother's room, I was going to turn round and leave. But I did not leave. I went back to the shoebox.'

Madam Gold nodded. 'Once it had brought you that far, it wasn't going to let you go without a fight. Your mother was a very determined woman. Ah! My friend was a tenacious woman!' She looked around the room with a sweeping smile that lingered for a moment on Mma as if she was the one whose tenacity Madam Gold was admiring.

Mma did not say a word in response. Nor did she return the smile. Instead, she said, 'All my life, I sacrificed for my mother. Why could she not meet me halfway?' Sacrifices. Sacrificial. Scarification. Mma enjoyed word-play. She had picked up the habit in primary school when the headmistress would begin every school day by throwing an alphabet to the pupils and asking them to make as many words as possible with it. She called it 'The Thinking Exercise'. Mma could make up many more S-words to describe her life.

'What do you know about sacrifice, eh, Mma?' Madam Gold asked. She was not wearing a wig. Her hair was corn-rowed but the braid was untidy, already loosening at the ends, and in front, tufts of hair sprang up. Mma's anger was still raw, hurting like fresh chilli rubbed into the eye.

'Aunty, you don't know what my childhood was like,' Mma said, even though Madam Gold had known her for as long as she could remember. She had been the only other constant in her life. She was trying not to cry. Not to remember. She did not want to remember children yelling 'ada ashawo' – whore's daughter – to her as she walked to school, children not much older than her throwing the words like missiles, and laughing as they struck her. Their cruelty was not gratuitous. It was calculated and consistent. It hit its mark and sent her to the privacy of the school toilets and to her bedroom to cry. She could not remember her life without the tears. She tried not to think of the words flailing in the air and then falling on her back to burn her, her skin welting. She tried not to think of the boys she did not know stopping her on the way from school to ask her how much she charged for her services – they had some cash to spend – while their friends tittered behind them, high-fiving each other, impressed by their daring.

'She told me I had no father! I was the only child in school without a father, dead or alive. Have you any idea how that made me feel?' Mma's voice remained flat. She did not wish to alienate Madam Gold by shouting.

Once, in anger, she had shouted at her mother, 'I bet you don't even know who my father is!' Casting the worst kind of aspersion on her, hoping that the accusation would force her into talking, into giving her a chance to seek the man out. But her mother had simply laughed that long laugh of hers and said, 'True, I don't know who he is. Are you happy now? You do not have a father. Kpom kwem. Onwe ife ozo?'

Madam Gold began to say something, stopped.

'Sorry?'

'I am sure it was not easy for you, but it was worse

for your mother. Your mother ... Did she tell you about Goody Goody and his wife? Eh? Did she?'

'No. Who are they?' She didn't mention them at all in her ... her memoirs. M was for memoirs. Trust her mother to exaggerate. She could not just write letters, it had to be a 'memoir', telling half-stories, sending her out in search of more. Sacrifice. Sacrificial. Scarificate. Skipping. Stories. Skipping stories. Snake. She listened to Madam Gold defend Ezi and said to herself, *My mother was a snake.* How ironic, she thought, that her mother was afraid of snakes.

'Snakes are dangerous creatures, that's why you can't have one,' her mother had told her when she had gone through a period of wanting a pet. She could not have a dog. 'Dogs need a lot of work. They need looking after like children. You have to walk them and clean up after them. Wipe up the pee, pick up the pooh. Huge responsibility.'

'A chicken, then?' In one of the story books she had, three English children had a pet hen called Hannah. Hannah had fluffy white feathers and a sharp beak. Mma imagined feeding it rice and letting it peck off her palm.

But no, not a chicken. 'Chickens you eat, you don't walk them. You fatten them and then you chop them up for soup. Have you ever seen anyone keep a chicken as a pet, eh?'

'A cat? Please.' She imagined a cuddly fluffy cat sleeping on her bed. A cat with black-and-white fur and a long tail. A cat she could stroke and carry around. 'Please, please, please, Mummy, a cat?'

'Only witches keep cats. Next thing you'll be wanting

a long broom to fly on. What's all this nonsense about, eh, Adamma? If you keep following me around like this while I'm trying to work, I'll trip over you!'

'A snake, then?' Snakes did not have to be walked. She was not sure how much they needed looking after but surely it could not be too difficult. She had imagined a snake in a cage, looping itself and raising its head to look at her. Maybe she could train it – get it to answer to its name, stick out its long tongue every time it was called.

'*Tufia!* What a crazy idea. Who keeps a snake as a pet? Have you gone completely mad? Snakes are evil. What will you be wanting next? The devil himself? *Tufia!*'

So, no dogs. No chickens. No cats. No snakes. Just a box with layers of dust and layers of stories.

'Who is Goody Goody?' Mma asked, thinking, What a name. Who would walk around with a name like that?

'Goody Goody was the devil,' Madam Gold said, hacking her words so that they fell harshly into the room. 'He. Was. The. Devil. *Heiii. Tufia.* The man *bu ekwensu ojo.* He was evil. He worked with his wife, who was worse than he was. She had the face of an angel, beautiful like a *mammywata,* but in her heart was evil. You'd think we women would help each other but not her. That woman was nasty. I am only telling you of Goody Goody so that you do not judge your mother too harshly. Are you listening to me? *I na-egekwa m nti, Adamma?*'

She waited for Mma to nod before she continued.

'She had to work for her money, unlike some people.' Madam Gold glared at her, daring her to say something.

Mma kept quiet. There was a short silence before Madam Gold sighed and continued.

'They were moneylenders, Goody Goody and his wife. He is long dead now, the man. Your mother was desperate. She had her rent to pay, you to feed and a business idea she was eager to put in motion. Talk about sacrifice! Don't you come talking to me about sacrifices because you don't know the half of what your mother went through for you!' Her voice rose as she spoke.

'You want to talk about sacrifice? Think of your mother!' Her chest heaved as if she were trying not to cry.

'Why did she go to a moneylender? Why not to a bank? Surely she had other choices. Nobody forced her to go to Goody Goody.'

Madam Gold hissed long and rolled her eyes. 'Choices, ke? Bank, ke? Why do you ask as if you did not grow up in this country? You think things have changed so much since the seventies? You think she did not try? You think you invented common sense and your mother had none? You children, you forget that no matter how high the okra tree grows, it's never mightier than the hand that planted it. You think you can ever be wiser than the womb that carried you?' Madam Gold shook her head and hissed again. 'Your mother, she carried you in her arms and went from one bank to the other, but not one would lend to a single woman with a baby and no collateral. Not one. And yet she still hoped to get her business off the ground. She had it all planned out, the enterprising woman that she was. Your mother had a lot of brains. First-class brains that woman had. She was going to supply the university with good-quality meat pies and sausage rolls and cakes, so that students and staff did not need to leave the campus at lunch. She was sure it would be successful. That way, she could stay home with you and earn at the same time. Why do you think she wanted that, eh? A job that kept her at home? You, Mma, guided her decisions. You and no one else. So don't talk to me about sacrifice because you don't know the half of what your mother suffered.

'She took a loan from Goody Goody and his wife, signed a contract, and invested in an oven. The business failed. Not for anything she had done, but because many others turned up as soon as she started. It was like a wildfire. Once she set up, a million others set up too. Women with no brains waiting to prey on someone else's idea. Competition became fierce and the others undercut her prices. She made her cakes with real butter – your mother was really into quality – and she was so optimistic. "People know quality," she'd tell me. "They appreciate quality and will pay for it." Well, it turned out people just wanted cheap snacks. They did not much care if the cake they were buying was made with real butter or dog piss as long as it had the right shape and a taste that was not too offensive. The competition used oil and could keep their prices low. Customers flocked to them. Your mother's real butter snacks sat untouched. And she still had a debt to settle. She went to Goody Goody's wife to beg her, woman to woman, to ask her husband for some more time. Goody Goody's wife promised her that if she did not pay up within two days, she should be prepared to face the conse-quences. Goody Goody was not a man to owe money to. I don't recall the exact details of the "consequences" but it involved you. You. Still want to talk about sacrifices?'

She hissed again; was Madam Gold blaming her for the choices her mother made? That's unfair, Mma thought, fuming silently.

'If she did not pay up within the agreed period, she had to pay with her daughter's life or something. There was a rumour that Goody Goody made his money by sacrificing children and no one doubted it. No one could touch him. He said that very often. Not even the policemen who hung around the secretariat near his moneylending office at lunchtime and turned a blind eye to the goings-on there could do anything to him. He had them in his pocket. There was no hiding from him. He used to say to defaulters, "No use trying to hide from me. I am a deity. I am everywhere." Your mother had to find a way to pay him back. What would you have done in her shoes? Tell me, Adamma, I'm listening. My ears are open, fill them up. What would you have done, eh?'

Shoes. Stranger. Strange. Her mother's shoes. A stranger's shoes. Her mother was a stranger. She was only finding that out now. It was easier to feel compassion for a stranger than for a strange mother. She was finding that out now, too. But compassion for a stranger who was also her mother was new. It was strange, and so she concentrated on something else, a feeling that was much more comfortable because it was normal. She asked, 'The men in shiny cars?'

'I'm telling you all this so that you do not judge her too harshly. There was nothing else she could do. She

21

was running out of time. Yes, there were a few men, but she . . . she was always proper. She was young, she was beautiful, she had a child and she was broke. There were all these men wanting to date her, so she had to choose carefully. She wanted a good life for you.'

Mma swallowed the question in her throat and asked instead, 'And my father? Do you know who my father was?'

She did not look at Madam Gold as she asked the question but stared straight ahead, concentrating on the two brilliant slits of light under the heavy curtains, drawn to keep the sun out.

'If your mother has written to you about all of these other things, Mma, do you not think that she will mention your father?'

'Aunty, the pages are too long. I don't have the patience to read through it all.'

'Shut up, Adamma! Shut that mouth up or may lightning solder it!' Madam Gold stood up and walked across the sitting room to where Mma was sitting. 'You come to me for neat answers, eh? You think your mother had anyone to give her that? You do not have the patience to read the writings of a dead woman, of your mother! Let me not hear such nonsense from you again. If I do, I swear, I'll walk you out of my house. You'll show respect for your mother here. Do you hear me? *I na-egekwa m nti?*'

'Yes, Aunty.'

Madam Gold panted as if from the effort of scolding Mma. She motioned for her to make room on the sofa and sat down next to her. No one said anything for a long while. Then she turned to Mma and gave her a long questioning look.

'I am sorry, Aunty.'

Madam Gold still had the ability to scare her into behaving, just as she had when Mma was a little girl, scared of the only woman who could tell her mother to shut up and get away with it.

'I'll tell you what you need to know but you have to read your mother's letters. It's the least you can do. You didn't even bury her properly, but what's done is done and I shall not go into that. Anyway . . .' She let the sentence hang and then got up. She walked to the curtains and drew them open.

3

On the first day, four weeks after Ezi died, there was a city-wide power cut. Mma sat in the sitting room and thought — as she often did when there was a power outage — of Mrs Nweke and one of the passages she used to make them recite in class: In the beginning God created the heaven and the earth. And the earth had no form. It was empty, covered with darkness and water. Then the Spirit of God hovered over the water, and God said, 'Let there be light,' and there was light. God saw that the light was good. Then He divided the light from the darkness. God called the light 'day', and the darkness he called 'night'. And the evening and the morning were the first day. On the first day, the earth was a formless wasteland, and darkness covered the abyss.

In primary-school Bible Knowledge class, Mma had to memorise them all: the seven days of creation. Mrs Nweke, always with a cane behind her back, drilled the lessons into her pupils.

She thought of Erinne, her best friend, and wished she were around. Erinne, of all the friends she had made and lost over the years, was the only one she could be open to. Erinne's mother had not stopped the two girls from being friends when they met in secondary school, even after meeting Ezi. Perhaps it was because Erinne's mother was a foreigner. She was a light-skinned Warri woman with a nose like a bird's beak. Maybe being away from home made her less nervous about her daughter's future prospects if she were seen to be fraternising with a girl of dubious parentage. Whatever her reasons, Mma was grateful to her. Whatever love might have belonged to Ezi, she transferred wholeheartedly to her friend's mother. She missed her now. And she wished Obi were around too.

Sometimes she thought of Obi as her first real boyfriend. He was not, of course, but he was the only one who had not been scared off by her mother. And that was something. No, that was more than something. That was 'big-big', as her mother would say, doubling words for emphasis, or just 'because-because'.

Ezi had not always been nice to Obi, peppering him with questions, asking if he intended to make an honest woman of her daughter, if he snored in his sleep, if he was stingy with money – and then laughing that rich laugh which bounced off the walls of the house as if it mocked everyone. The more awkward Obi appeared, the longer she stretched out the laughter like a rubber band – when you thought it had reached breaking point and would snap, it recoiled and started all over again. When Mma tried to apologise he waved it off and told her she could hardly be blamed for who her mother was, she had absolutely nothing to say sorry for.

This year, she and Obi had planned to spend the Christmas holidays together in Enugu. She, because she had nowhere else to go. No village that she knew of. No family inviting her for boisterous get-togethers with feasts of goat meat and fried chicken and jollof rice garnished with moi-moi. He, because he wanted to spend more time with her. It was the only time of the year he got three uninterrupted weeks to do as he pleased. And what it would please him to do this year, he told her, was to spend it with her.

'I want to be at your service,' he had said. 'Every single day for three weeks. No rushing off. No deadlines to meet. Nothing.' He would go nowhere near the chambers where he worked as a junior solicitor. She had happily agreed to make whatever arrangements suited her, for the both of them.

Three weeks to do with as he pleased, as long as his mother agreed. One phone call telling him he was expected home in Onitsha for Christmas, and he was gone.

'I'm sorry, Mma, but my mother says I've got to be there. Nneka, my cousin, is getting married and every-one's returning for it. Even my uncle and his Caribbean wife are coming all the way from London for it.'

'Are they walking from London?' She could not keep the sarcasm from her voice.

'There's no need to be like that, sweetheart.' He held her around the waist and kissed her.

Mma knew she could have sulked and thrown a tantrum like a spoilt child but it would change nothing. If it had not been Nneka's wedding, there would have been something else. There always would be. As long as they were only boyfriend and girlfriend, she would always play second fiddle to his family. She knew it had nothing to do with his love for her, but that was very little comfort. Obi loved her, but duty was duty. It was as simple as that. She ought to understand. Duty was often stronger than love.

But understanding did not help her, when she thought of being left behind. Abandoned, stuck in the house on Neni Street to see out the languorous December days alone. Families could be a yoke around one's neck. She, more than anyone else, should know this. After all, she had had to live with her mother.

'Couldn't I maybe go with you?' she asked recklessly, kissing the side of his neck.

'Don't be silly, Mma. Who would I say you were?' Not much taller than she was, he nuzzled into her braids. He spat out a strand of hair that had got into his mouth and kissed her back.

'Indeed,' she said, wishing she could say more, but she lacked the courage to do so. It was the sort of thing her mother would have done and she was nothing like her mother, thank goodness for that.

Don't be silly, Mma. Who would I say you were? The words replayed in her head all of that day and for days after; in unguarded moments she found herself hurting with a new pain from a conversation that, as far as Obi was concerned, was over and done with. Her life was a wasteland. And how often had she imagined ways to transform it? To till it and nurture something green and beautiful?

The house, number 11, was near-empty. Only one other apartment was still occupied. The family (a widower and his four children) had been planning to drive down to their village a few hundred kilometres from Enugu for the New Year. The oldest son was preparing for his university entrance exams and was still

27

having extra lessons from a retired physics teacher who lived nearby. He put the boy through rigorous exercises that pleased his concerned father but made the son melancholic. Every time Mma saw him, he looked like he was about to cry. Getting into medical school was a lot more important than spending Christmas with distant relatives, even if this was the year that had been planned for him and his cousins to undergo the rites of passage to become men. There was going to be a big family celebration, with goats slaughtered and bags of rice cooked, enough to feed the entire village. Everyone in the family had returned, even relatives who lived as far away as Kafanchan and Maiduguri, for whom the trip to the east was too far to be made annually.

'They'll understand,' the widower told Mma, as though he needed her to cleanse him of his guilt. Mma, who had never had any family, distant or close, had no response. It was only the years of training herself to be restrained – to not be as brash as her mother – that stopped her from asking, 'Do you think I care?'

She watched the morose young man for whom the visit 'home' had been cancelled and felt no pity. She listened to his father complain about the sacrifice and her heart was not moved. It was this sense of tradition, of loyalty to family, that was keeping her lonely now. Full of self-pity, she had no strength to spare on someone else's problems.

The heat had become unbearable. There was no air-conditioned relief inside the house. There was no TV to distract her and keep her mind from returning to the papers in a box under her mother's bed.

Escaping the heat of the living room she sat on the balcony, rubbing her temples, trying to keep a headache at bay. She rested her head on the railing, one palm on her chin, the other swallowed in the folds of her dress. Her mind was a whirlwind gathering thoughts and scattering them so that she almost felt dizzy. She found it difficult to focus on any one thought and she blamed the dream for this, too, for this restlessness that had taken hold of her. And the dream was also to be blamed for her thoughts returning, no matter how far away they went, to a certain cupboard in the kitchen.

She picked the day's *Times* off the floor and began to fan herself with it. The paper, limp from the heat, flapped as it went swish-swish across her face, bringing little relief. Nothing was going right for her this month. This sort of heat was not normal for December. If this is what global warming is all about, she thought, then we are in for big, big trouble.

Yesterday on TV, in between blackouts, an evangelist had warned that global warming was an intimation of the fires of hell. Every day, he said, the world was getting closer to the end, when it would erupt in a great ball of fire and the holy would be raptured but the others would be condemned to eternal damnation in hell to roast with the devil, the father of sins himself. Her catholic sensibilities prevented her from believing in predictions from TV pastors, but still she could not wonder if there was not a grain of truth in what he said. 'This heat is not normal,' she said, fanning herself harder.

There was a knock. For a minute she thought it might be Obi, defying his family to spend time with her like they had planned. She dropped the newspaper and ran

29

to open the door. It was her neighbour's son. She held the door half-open.

'What?'

'Good evening. Sorry to disturb you, but, em . . . we have run out of matches. Em . . .'

'You want to borrow a box of matches?' She could tell he was embarrassed, having to come and ask. At his age he had to be.

His nod was barely perceptible in the dark, reminding her that she had to light her lanterns too. What must he think of her, sitting in the dark? She felt her way into the kitchen, lit a lantern, left it on the sitting-room table, and returned through the doorway with a box for the boy.

'You can keep it, Izu.'

'Thank you.' His teeth flashed white in the dark, then he turned and half ran down the stairs to his flat.

Mma felt a kinship with him. She had lived her entire life in embarrassment. She knew what it felt like, even on a small scale like Izu's. If there was one gift her mother had unwittingly left her, it was a sense of solidarity with sufferers. They were her real family. Not her mother, who was the reason Mma started to have upside-down thoughts. The first time she had one, she articulated it, telling her mother, 'I wish you were dead!' And quick as lightning, her mother had slapped her on her mouth.

'If I ever hear such upside-down words from you again, I'll kill you! Is there something wrong-wrong with your head? Are your brains upside-down? *Isi omebili gi?*'

Mma, fifteen and stunned by her mother's vehemence, went howling into her bedroom. Her mother usually

30

laughed off her daughter's outbursts, the same as she did with her anxieties. She liked to think it was the shock of it, the unexpectedness, which made her cry, for at fifteen and curved in all the necessary places, you did not cry for being beaten, did you? But she had also sworn to herself that her mother would never make her cry again.

Mma slapped off a mosquito that had landed on her forehead. Almost immediately, a second one perched on her right ear. The last thing she needed, she thought to herself, was to fall ill with malaria. The illness always left her drained. The last time she had it, her mother had forced Sprite down her throat to keep her energy up. She should go to bed, she thought, although the last thing on her mind was sleep. She did not want a repeat of the dream. But her bedroom was mosquito-proof: it had treated nets over the door and windows. She got up, picked up the lantern from the sitting-room table and made for her room. She got to her door and turned back.

While her mother was alive, Mma had avoided entering her room. Now she was shocked to see how little it had changed since her childhood when she would sneak in to snuggle against the sweet warmth of her body. The massive bed with a wrought-iron head was still where it always was, opposite the door. She had loved it as a child, sitting against the head and pretending it was a throne. For years she dreamt of owning a bed like it. The bedspread was different, but typical. Vibrant yellow-and-red dots on a background of green, a spread of flowers she could not identify, on a huge expanse of grass – not something Mma would have chosen, but her mother had always surrounded herself with such bright patterns. Mma preferred muted colours, monotones that did not attract any attention: beiges and greys that slunk into the shadows. That was the sort of life she wished she had led. It would have been easier to make and keep friends that way. She would have been happy staying in the background, letting others lead, as long as it guaranteed her a lifetime of happiness. But no matter how quiet she kept, her mother thrust them both into the light. With that laughter and that loud voice of hers, no one could ignore her. Ah, in her next incarnation, may she be struck mute, Mma thought uncharitably.

The walnut dresser was still in its usual position beside the bed; bottles of perfume standing in line as if waiting patiently for their owner to waltz in and spritz them on. Beside the door was an enormous cupboard, mahogany brown with a frieze of carved flowers and tangled vines across its front. Mma imagined it swollen to bursting. As a little girl she had enjoyed rummaging in the cupboard, going through her mother's clothes just for the sheer pleasure of it. How glamorous she had thought her mother then.

Leaning against the wall were two recent additions to the room: two framed photographs of her mother which Mma had asked Obi to move from the sitting room into the bedroom. She had assumed Obi would just push them under the bed, not prop them up as if people would come in to admire them. She had always felt confronted by the larger-than-life pictures. In a house where there was no visible male presence, the huge, framed photographs were all the more telling of the sort of woman Ezi was. Mma could have destroyed the photographs now, with her mother grinning at her from one of them, her hands artistically folded under her chin to reveal long, shiny red nails, her gapped teeth visible – she was not sure why she had not. Perhaps because no matter what she felt for her mother, she did not want to desecrate an image of the dead. It was one thing to refuse their last will, but it was another to purposefully destroy the image of a person who was kin to you. She did not know what she would do if she moved house because there was no way she would take the pictures. Maybe she would leave them here on Neni Street, let the new owner dispose of them. Or offer them to Madam Gold. There was still time to decide. No need to get all worked up now.

She looked around the room, trying not to think of the days when she would wake from a nightmare and run to her mother. Lying next to her, taking in the smell of her back, her nose pressed tightly against its warm softness, was enough to calm her fears. No need to think about those days either. A few good memories could not cancel out a lifetime of bad ones. She remembered one night when she woke up trembling from a bad dream and her mother's door was locked and no matter how much she stood at the door and cried and begged, her mother would not let her in. 'Go away, Mma, you're a big girl now. No need to come into my bed.'

'Please, Mummy.'

'No, go away, you silly-silly girl.'

'*Biko*, Mummy. Please. Please. Please.'

'*Mba*. Go. Away. Go-go. Silly-silly girl!'

In the morning she had seen a man with oversized

glasses leave the house, his shoes in his hands, tiptoeing, trying not to make a noise for fear of alerting the little girl, not realising that he had already been seen. She never asked her mother to let her into her bed again, no matter the magnitude of her nightmares. Her mother began to complain that she lurked-lurked in corners like a stranger.

Had this been a normal family, Mma thought, she would have had to sort out her mother's belongings, take the things she cherished and distribute the rest to her family. She would have kept her mother's red shoes for sentimental reasons. But her mother had no family that she knew of. No sisters to inherit her flamboyant skirts and multicoloured tie-dye boubous; no aunties to inherit her jewellery. Probably for the best there's no family. She was not entirely convinced any other person would appreciate her mother's love for the colourful and the showy. Her earrings were big and gaudy. Her brooches looked like miniature weapons of torture. Mma was sure that the pendant her mother was wearing when she went into hospital, a long contraption shaped like an arrow, was sharp enough to cut off a head. Not the sort of thing people were eager to inherit. The hospital had given it to her, sealed in a plastic bag with her mother's rings and bracelet. And Mma hadn't even brought them home. She had dropped them into the begging bowl of a young woman outside the hospital gates, wishing her a Merry Christmas, even though it was only November. She smiled now as she remembered the beggar biting on the huge gold bracelet. Hopefully, the woman was able to sell them and buy some tins of milk for the baby she was carrying. Mma had no use for them. And this act was sure to infuriate her mother's spirit. Let her have a taste of everything she had put Mma through.

Mma knelt on the floor and felt under the bed for the box. She dragged it out, freeing clouds of dust that flew into her nose and sent her into a sneezing fit. She traced her name on the cover, traced Obi's, drew a flying arrow between them and told herself that she was not stalling for time, she could do this. Her mother, after all, could not hurt her any more. The shoebox was taped with black heavy-duty Scotch tape; she would need to cut it loose. She put the box down and went into the kitchen for a pair of scissors.

She opened the scissors and used the tip of one blade to slit the tape. She felt a sense of dread. She knew instinctively that once she started reading the letters, something would change in her life. For the better, or for the worse. She expected that it would be the latter. She could not imagine that anything that had to do with her mother would be good for her.

She sank into the bed and lifted the lid. Inside were several sheets of loose paper. Not the letters she had expected, but what seemed to be a manuscript of some sort. The papers had the stale smell of age. How appropriate, Mma thought, that anything her mother touched would be defiled, destined to decay, so that letters written not so long ago smelt like they had come out of a different era. But when she took a handful from the box, she was surprised that they did not feel old to the touch: they did not feel all feathery and light from age, and they were not frayed at the sides like old sheets are.

Instead, they were stiff, full of the virility of the young and packed with urgent lines, sometimes slanting, sometimes straight. In some places the writing was like chicken scratchings, all joined together so that Mma thought she would never be able to make sense of it. Her mother had always prided herself on her beautiful handwriting. Mma found it almost impossible to believe that this was hers. She dropped the paper back in the box, closed the lid and walked towards the door.

That was the first day.

4

D Mma often imagined D as short and assertive. Extend D and it sounds like a groan. D stands for dark. And for death. D is for death coming from unexpected quarters. Sometimes death has a smell to it. It smells like the perfume her mother wore on her last day. It smells like otapiapia in your nostrils and you being unable to sneeze it out. Death is not dark like it is pictured in books. It is a *mélange* of bright, bold colours.

Did her mother know she was going to die? Had she felt a quickening of her breath that morning as she took a bath and thought, This is my last bath? And the night before she went to bed, had she silently said her goodbyes to all the things she held dear? Mma saw a programme once where a woman said that on the day her husband died, he had set out all his ties and shoes on the bed and held each one to his nose. When his wife asked him why he was doing it, he couldn't explain. He said he felt a compulsion to. Later that day he was killed in a freak accident while he was playing football: a goalpost fell on him and fractured his skull. The woman looked into the camera and said, 'I have often thought what death feels like, what my husband felt at that moment he was transiting.' Mma had thought her choice of word interesting. *Transiting*. Now, though, she under-stood it was the woman's way of consoling herself. Death was not an end. What would it be like to die? Mma thought now. What would it feel like? Would it be like a floating and a flying and a looking back and regretting what you had not done? Perhaps when dead people regret, when they leave a life unfinished, like a house unbuilt, their spirits roam the earth and they die a second death, a death worse than their first.

The day Ezi died, Madam Gold told Mma between heaving sobs, 'You know the worst thing about your mother dying? It was too sudden! I didn't even get a chance to tell her all the things I wanted to tell her.'

Mma thought of the two women as joined at the hips. Madam Gold was always at their house, the only one who gave Mma the semblance of having a proper family. Her three children were older than Mma, much older, but when they were younger, they had sometimes accompanied their mother to visit. Mma called them her cousins. They were married now and dispersed all over the country, she had not seen them in many years, but Madam Gold was a constant. What else could they still have to say to each other after all the years of talking? 'There were still so many things I never got to tell her! And you . . . what you did . . .'

Mma fought the urge to ask Madam Gold what was so bad about what she did. Madam Gold might have had a lot to talk to her mother about; for her, it was the opposite. She and her mother were all 'talked out'. They had nothing new to say to each other. It had been like that for years. The silence between them had never been awkward because it was their normal routine. Death just stamped that silence with permanence. At the beginning, she had thought it was just as well.

D is for death. Death is like a thief in the night. She remembered that from a homily. The priest had said that death steals away its victims, dragging them helplessly to the grave. He had made death sound like a skilful criminal, the sort who could pinch a wallet from a front pocket without the victim ever realising until the crime was long committed and the offender safely gone, very much like the Artful Dodger in *Oliver Twist*, Mma thought. But her mother had not acted like a person who had something precious stolen away. The more Mma thought of it, the more convinced she was that her mother had had a premonition, that she had been aware that death was coming for her. Some people do, after all. Obi had told her about his grandmother, who, as a young girl, had been sent to live with a family in another village. She shared a room in the house with the aged mother of her mistress, a room with one small window and no light at night once the candle was blown out.

'My grandmother said that the old woman smelt too much of death,' Obi said. 'It scared her to spend night after night in that room. One day, this old woman, who could barely leave her bed, got up before dawn and started sweeping the room. My grandmother said that the stench of death was so strong that she ran out of the room to the front yard. She was still there, under a tree, when she heard shrieks from the house. The woman had died.'

Mma was convinced that her mother must have felt her imminent death in her bones or in the air. The day before her mother went into hospital, she had stood over Mma, sprawled on the sitting-room sofa, reading a novel.

'If anything should happen to me, I want you to read these,' her mother had said, handing her a huge shoebox with 'Size 41' plastered across it as if that was the brand of the shoe itself. Mma had barely looked up from her book. Nobody said something like that unless they knew, for certain, that something would happen. But that was not how Mma had thought of it then. 'Seeing as you love to bury your nose in thick books all day, reading-reading as if you were a professor, I'm providing you with enough material to last you a long-long time.' Her mother had chuckled and then, her tone turning serious, added, 'Should the worst happen—'

'Oh, Mummy, stop being so melodramatic,' Mma had cut in, upset at being disturbed. She was forced to look up from the book. Her thumb marked the page she was on. 'You're not going in for open-heart surgery. It's only your appendix. There is nothing "should the worst happen" about it!'

Nobody was scared of having their appendix removed, she had told her mother. 'Doctors will tell you it's the easiest surgery to perform! Obi's cousin had his appendix removed in the dark – the hospital generator was not working and the doctor had a nurse shine a torch for him while he did it.' It was a job even the otapiapia peddler could do while singing his famous *ife na-ata gi si gi n'aka, onye ata na chukwu uta*. Otapiapia killed everything from bedbugs to mice.

And now, she tried not to think of the white poison tucked away in a corner of the kitchen cupboard, far away from the jars of crayfish and ground melon-seed.

It was as lethal to humans as it was to the pests that ran amok in many kitchens.

She had not accepted the box, had not even looked at it when her mother had put it down noisily on the sitting-room table and gone back to her room, muttering that the cramps, worrying-worrying her were nothing worse than a diseased appendix. Mma had convinced herself that they were nothing too, for as her mother said, 'You lie-lie too many times, you begin to think it's the truth.'

The truth was like a prism. That was the lesson she learnt from Mr Ogene. When Mma was thirteen, her Form Two science teacher, the enthusiastic Mr Ogene, nicknamed 'Einstein' for his legendary science skill, brought the most magical thing she had ever seen to class. It was a block wrapped in a knotted handkerchief which he unwrapped with great ceremony, wiped on his shirt and held out to the class. It sparkled gloriously. He positioned it at various angles and asked the enchanted students what colour they thought it was. Then he drawled in his deep baritone, 'The colours produced by a prism are due to different refraction rates. And so it is with the truth. There are different shades to it, and whichever shade one gets is reliant on the angle one is looking at it from.'

Einstein believed in blending science with the 'facts of life', to keep his young pupils interested. 'Science is not abstract; it's about life. It's about what you eat, what you wear. It's about how you live. It's as much about the absurdities of life as it is about its pleasures,' he said. Sometimes, what he said made sense to his young acolytes. Sometimes, it did not. But like most of her classmates, Mma's attention never swayed. Einstein's classes stayed with her. Years after she left school, she could still reproduce, line by line, whole sentences of his lessons. So now, at almost twenty-two, she found solace in the words of her former teacher. If there was no absolute truth, then there was no absolute lie. And so she had not lied. She had just shaded her truth and that had helped push the memory of what she had thought of doing to the very bottom of her heart where it saw no light. It was imprisoned – as secrets we do not wish to remember often are – in the dark hidden places to dwell with other forgotten things: the name of the shy classmate whose face is almost hidden in the school photograph; the doll we played with every day when we were young, or the dark thoughts we have tried hard to un-remember. In fact, she had almost forgotten about it, hardly ever thought of it until the dreams began. And then she was forced to go through the clutter of that dark place, to pull out that secret, dust off its cobwebs and examine it, to consider what to do with it. (What exactly did one do with a secret whose veracity one could no longer guarantee? And which once known was sure to ruin one's chances of happiness?) It was not something she could tell Obi. And certainly not Erinne, the only one who had stood by her all those years. There were just some things one never shared, not even with those who had proven to be the type of friends to stick by one through thick and thin. The price was higher, far too high than she was prepared to pay. And what she did; well, that was done. She could not begin to regret it now.

5

Her mother's letters to her were titled 'My Memoirs; The Truth about My Life'. The words, written neatly in black, were underlined twice in red ink, like thin wavy trails of blood.

Red ink dancing on paper. The stark contrast of red, black and white. Her mother's cursive, a work of art to be envied. 'They don't teach kids to write any more,' her mother had often complained. 'In our day,' she said then, 'we had to actually learn cursive. These days kids write like they're scratching in the sand. You can't make any sense of it.' On the first day, Mma began to read. An elegantly slanting W.

My darling Daughter,
Where? Where to start? Where does one start writing about one's life? I never thought it would be difficult to write about my life: it is, after all, my life. Who better to tell it than myself? Now I have started and I find it is almost impossible knowing where to begin. Should I start with your birth? You are a part of my life, after all. And in a a way, everything started with your birth. If you had never come along, things might have turned out differently, I might have made other choices.

43

But I wonder. Should I start from my birth? That's when my father would start, in any case. Let me start with my birth. That is perhaps, more than your birth, the beginning. The beginning-beginning.

I was born on a Saturday, the oldest of four children. Why is this important? My father believed it explained everything. Why I did what I did. Why I was the way I was. My father, Christian and superstitious, blamed it all on the day of my birth. 'The last day of creation! The day He created animals. No wonder you are the way you are!' Those were the last words he spoke to me. The words I have carried with me all these years and sometimes I have wondered if he had a point.

My father said I acted like a bull because I was created alongside the bulls. The mud out of which I was moulded must have come from the mud under their feet.

My mother, not as Christian as my father, blamed it on the carelessness of my personal chi, my personal god. 'Your chi went off to frolic and have a drink the day you were made. It's your bad luck. That's why you're a torture to me. May your own children bring you as much unhappiness as you've brought me. That's all I can wish you, if you insist on being headstrong.'

Maybe her curse did come true. A mother's curse is a terrible thing, even if it is not justified. What I had done was not so bad, I said to her. The blame and the curses belonged to someone else. Not to me.

'You have the yam, you have the knife. You decide who gets fed.' I am a bit like my mother. When my mind is made up, there is no shifting it. It sits like a pillar of solid gold and it would take only the heat of a fire to melt it.

She failed to see that I had neither the yam nor the knife. Both had been wrested from me. I was following the only route I could, especially with you to think of, too. I had hoped that she would see it. I had hoped that my friends would. In the end only Madam Gold remained. She, the friend of my heart, has stuck by me closer than a sister. Where are my blood siblings? My sister and my two brothers? They would not forgive me for ruining their chances. For making our parents unhappy. For having our family pointed out. When a finger dips in palm oil, it soils the entire hand. You were not my only responsibility. My entire family was too.

'You won't even think of your sister who still has to marry,' my mother accused. 'Your brothers. You're a wicked, wicked child. Wicked and selfish. You think only of yourself. You would not think even of your baby.' All the while she scolded me, I could see how hard she was trying not to break down, not to cry. She tied and untied her headscarf, clapped her hands in my face and I was afraid that she would lose control and strike me. I do not know if I would not have hit her back. Then there would have been hell.

When she died, my father sent word that I was not allowed to come to her funeral. I had killed her, he said. 'You did not spring from my loins!' The emissary was a nervous woman who would not look me in the face, as if she would contract whatever it was I was cursed with. I asked her about the others – my siblings – but she rushed out as if a dog was at her heels. I laughed. And laughed.

Sometimes I think of my siblings, I wonder where they are. I secretly hope that when I am gone, they will hear and be sorry and seek you out. I do not want to think that they have forgotten all about me, that all the years we spent together as a family mean nothing in the face of my decision. Blood is thicker than water, you hear. Ha! Let me tell you, some blood flows thinner. And some water is as thick as sludge. Think of Madam Gold. Which sister can be closer than she who has stuck by me all these years? Of all the friends I made, she was the only one not to abandon me. The only aunt you have ever known. I wish you a friend like her. A sister like her. She is a gift from the gods. I have always been able to count on her friendship. I don't know what I'd have done without her. She does not always agree with the choices I make but she will never stop being my friend. She stood up to her husband for me. She told him our friendship meant more to her than any other. He is not happy-happy with this but he will not oppose it. She says she will never forget what I did for her, but what I did was very small, insignificant almost. She has repaid me many times over. Did I ever tell you how we met? I don't think so. First let me tell you about your other aunt and uncles. The ones who share your blood.

Your Uncle Emma is three years younger than

I. We called him 'Sugar Boy' because as a kid he constantly stole sugar cubes from the kitchen cupboard. I daren't think about the state of his teeth now. My mother used to tell him he'd pay for all that sugar in his old age. He was very smart. The last time I saw him, he had just graduated with a second-class upper in biochemistry from Ibadan. He should have a good job now. It is difficult to imagine Sugar Boy as a middle-aged man. He must be married, his own kids. It is different for men. My mud would not stick on him. As long as he's got himself a good job – and surely he must have – he can get a well-brought-up girl from a good home to marry. I wonder if he has children? I wonder if he thinks of me. I wonder if he tells them about me. And if he does, what he tells them.

Your Uncle Jerry, your Uncle Jerry . . . What is there to say about him? The baby of the family. He came six years after Sugar Boy and solidified my mother's place in her husband's home. One son is good but two makes your position unassailable. No one can question it. What Jerry wants, Jerry gets. That was how it was when we were growing up. He was almost like my baby, too. I remember wiping his bottom. I remember the day my mother came back from the hospital with him. I held out a finger and he grasped it tight. From that moment onwards he became mine. He usurped Sugar Boy's place as my shadow. I spoilt him. We all did. Jerry was a beautiful baby and it was impossible to refuse him anything. But he did not raise a voice in my defence. Maybe he would have helped my parents change

47

their minds about kicking me out. But he was a student at the time. Young and fighting for his own place in life, I suppose. He was an economics student at Ife. He is probably working in a bank, if he makes it out of bed on time. My mother had to cajole him up every morning to go to school. Sometimes, I'd have to feed him in bed. He was spoilt with a capital S. I pity his wife. I suppose his life has proceeded normally too.

I have left my sister for last. She is the one I miss the most, and the one whose chances I have ruined. I feel guilty about it. Sometimes. It wasn't easy, believe me. It was not. But I had you to think of. Between a daughter and a sister, the competition is stiff, but an offspring always wins. Kelechi is four years younger than Sugar Boy. She looked up to me. Kelechi was beautiful. My mother called her *Enenebeejghiolu* and really, you could tell, even at a young age, that she had the sort of beauty that was capable of keeping many men away from work. She has a mole above her right eye and the whitest teeth you would ever find. But what was all that beauty worth if she had to pay for my sins? I know what I have most likely put her through, but my parents left me no choice. I had hoped that my mother would understand. It would have been a lot less bad if she had supported me and allowed me to live at home. Maybe I would have rethought. Maybe I would have gone back to Kaduna. I don't know. And all the while, I had to think of you. In the long run, it was maybe a good thing they did what they did, forcing me to stick to my decision;

you see, once they sent me out of their home, there was no way I could go back, tail between my legs. How could I have lived with myself then? I don't suppose they expected me to carry out my threat to live alone, to bring you up alone, knowing how much I loved Kelechi and how much my decision would affect the way she was viewed, the remarks she more than my brothers would have had to face. You know how our people are, I do not need to tell you.

Sometimes in life, we have to take a stand. It does not help to sit on the fence, even if we have to hurt the people we love-love. That is what I want you to remember. If I have taught you anything, I want it to be that. I don't want to imagine how it would have been for me had I gone back to Kaduna. Yet there were days at the beginning when the temptation was so strong that I packed up, dressed you and went to the park to board a taxi to Kaduna. It was only the voice in my ear whispering unbearable things that stopped me from returning to the city I had abandoned. I look at you sometimes and I wonder how things would have been for you, for me, if I had followed through my plans on those days.

Letters dancing on paper. One letter joined another and that one joined another and they formed words. Sometimes the handwriting seemed jumpy. Excited. Angry. Other times they retained the serenity they had at the beginning. Words on paper. And the words formed stories. Her head stuffed up with the history she was unearthing. She had grandparents. An aunt. Uncles. Possibly cousins. She needed a drink. She went to the kitchen, poured herself a whisky and downed it in one. With the alcohol burning sweetly in her throat, she went back to her mother's bedroom and continued reading.

When I said I had three siblings, I lied. There is a fourth, a boy, Independence. Indy for short.

Mma snorted. Lying was second nature to her mother; Mma was not surprised. More family crawling out of the pages to make her acquaintance, freed from her mother's lies. Prison. Prism. Purse your lips together and release a perfect P.

But this is all depressing. I want some sun-sun. Some laughter. Some heaven-heaven to break into this sad-sad story. Every memoir has happiness. Even this. I must have some warmth.

Let me move things up and start from Enugu. Not the Enugu you know, Mma, but the Enugu of a lonely woman's memories. Enugu in the eighties was a beautiful city. People had picnics in parks and went dancing on Friday nights. The Polo Park was well maintained. The lawn was green and tidy, nothing at all like the jungle it is now, where mad men piss-piss everywhere and children on their way from school get rid of their empty cans and wrappers. That is how it is now, not so? Before-before, when I first moved to Enugu, Polo Park was so clean you could eat off the grass. I took you there sometimes to go on the swings and the see-saw. Do you remember? What is left of it now? The merry-go-round that has ceased to work and weeds where flowers used to be.

That is the problem with this country. We like good things but we do not want to put in the effort to keep them good. Government property is nobody's father's and so must be allowed to rot. People with the money run to London and America. At some point, our country was as good as all the foreign-foreign ones. We are even running to Ghana now. Yet we once hosted Ghanaian refugees. Now even it has overtaken us. It's the new Europe. Newly-weds go on honeymoon to Ghana.

I have veered off course, talking about Ghana and refugees when I set out to talk about Enugu. There was Lobito's boutique where I shopped. He's dead now, Lobito, gunned down by robbers. Some said they were not robbers but assassins, hired by a jealous competitor. Nobody really knows the truth but what does it matter, he is dead. That's all that is of importance. That someone stole his life. The end result is the same, not so?

You should have seen me then, in my imported ready-made clothes from Lobito. I turned heads at cocktail parties. Even when other women sneered at me, it was always with a hint of envy, a desire to be me. Women are like that. Always wanting what isn't theirs to want in the first place. Is it nature, you think? Yes, they might all have looked happy and satisfied, but I knew better than most that marriage and happiness don't often go hand in hand. They are like oil and water, except in soup, and how many marriages are like soup?

Mma only stopped when she heard her neighbour's door bang. Surely she could not have been reading all night? She got up and peered out of her mother's window into the compound behind theirs. She was surprised to see the early-morning sun bursting through the mango trees in the yard. But she was not feeling sleepy. What she felt was hunger. She ventured to see Mama Ekele-of-the-ample-breasts. She had a roadside spot not too far from the house, from which she sold fried yam and mouth-watering akara balls. Mma hoped she had not been seized by the going-home mania. She needed food in her stomach, she needed the strength to continue reading.

6

Mama Ekele was there but there were no customers. She was big: the woman's breasts looked like they could feed all the babies in Enugu and still not slacken. She boasted often of how she had nursed not only her nine children, but her cousin's twins as well. 'I nursed three babies at the same time and still had milk left over!'

'The woman has breasts like the udders of a cow,' Mma's mother had laughed once. 'Does she throw them over her shoulders when she takes a shower?' Mma, who as a rule disapproved of her mother's mockery, had refused to laugh, even though she did find the image rather funny.

'Your eye,' the woman said.

'*Anya na ibe ya*,' Mma greeted. 'How is business?'

'You've seen now. What shall it be?'

'Four balls of akara and three pieces of yam.'

'Is that all you're eating? You young girls of nowadays, always concerned with your weight. A woman should be full so that when a man holds her, he is holding more than air. How will you nurse babies with no weight, eh? My cousin, a nurse in Ngwo, when she had her baby . . .' As she talked, she reached out for a tuber of yam beside her. Her breasts heaved as she expertly

53

sliced it and threw four pieces into a bowl of water. She screamed a name and one of her numerous children dashed out. She asked her to fetch a box of matches.

'I haven't had a customer all morning,' she said.

'The morning is still young. It's not even six thirty yet.'

'Ha! It's got nothing to do with the age of the morning, oo. I've been here since five. Yesterday I had maybe ten, twelve customers. How am I going to buy Christmas dress and shoes for my children? Christmas goat is out of the question. No *ngwongwo* this year at all. My cousin the nurse, skinny like a sugarcane stalk, I asked her . . .' Mma switched off.

The mention of *ngwongwo* reminded her of Erinne. She had been invited to spend the Christmas holiday with her and her family in their village. Erinne was from Ngwo, not too far from Enugu, but having made plans of her own with Obi, Mma had turned down the invitation. 'There will be plenty of *ngwongwo*, oo,' Erinne had promised, hoping to entice Mma with her favourite dish. 'As much goat head as you can finish.' Now that her plans were changed, she was free to go. Erinne would be more than happy to see her, but she feared that she might have been invited out of pity; she knew how busy Erinne's family would be entertaining guests, her father was a chief or something. She did not know if she would be able to keep up the pretence of a mourning daughter. When she called Erinne to tell her of her mother's death, Erinne had gently chided her, 'You sound so clinical about it, like you had a bad tooth pulled out.'

'How else should I be about it, Erinne?'

'You must feel something – she was your mother. She is your mother.'

'Ha! Your mother is more of a mother to me than *she* ever was. Why should I start pretending now, *biko?*'

'Don't talk like this to Mummy, oo.'

'Of course not, ooo. I dey craze?'

Erinne's mother was big on respect for one's parents. But she has earned the right to be so, Mma often thought. My mother has not. Still, she knew she had to fake some sense of loss. And she had managed to. But it would be difficult to keep it up for longer than a few hours.

The oil hissed and formed bubbles on top of the akara and yam frying in the pan, and Mama Ekele-of-the-ample-breasts turned them over with a humongous spoon. 'So . . . when is your mother's burial?'

'She's been buried already.' Mma's voice was curt. It had both the sting and the dryness of pepper. She was certain that the food-seller knew her mother had already been buried. The ambulance had come into their street first and made a short stop for the corpse to say its goodbyes, before continuing on to the cemetery, its siren – as was customary – wailing loudly and dragging excited children out of their homes. Besides, many of the families inhabiting number 11 bought their Sunday breakfasts from Mama Ekele, and Mma was sure they talked. This woman just wanted an excuse to scold her, to chide her for burying her mother quickly and quietly like a pauper when everybody knew how rich she had been. Mma was sure Mama Ekele felt cheated out of a good party. None of the women who now gossiped about how quickly her mother had been buried had cared for her. No matter what one thought of Ezi, if she died she was to be buried in style. You expended your finances and borrowed if you must, you hired women versed in the act of crying; professional mourners to shout and wail (like those who could not or would not cry loud enough did), you threw a party lasting for at least two days to ensure that she got the kind of send-off worthy of someone whose womb housed you. You made sure people ate and people drank until they could take no more. It did not matter what was thought of her, you would have to do your duty. That was simply the way things worked. Mma had denied her mother this. Madam Gold had told her that such a deed could not go unpunished, as the earth to which her mother was returning to its womb was a woman. 'Nature will find a way to take its revenge.' Her words had fallen on Mma's ears and bounced right back like an echo.

'You've wronged your mother, Mma. You wouldn't even—' And she had stopped because she could not continue without crying. She could wash her friend's corpse, she could dress it, but only kin could decide how it was buried. Mma did not see the need to pretend. Everybody knew that her mother had left her enough money to bury her properly, and so if she did not, it was a matter of choice. She did not care what they thought of her, she knew that all she wanted was to excise herself from her mother. Surely they understood that, these women who had kept their daughters away from Mma's house, who had whispered about Mma's mother, who had pitied Mma for being fated to be her mother's daughter.

The food-seller did not say another word. She gave the yam slices one more rapid turn in the pan and scooped them out, shaking the excess oil back into the pan and wrapping them up in a newspaper.

'Pepper or salt?' she said grudgingly. She should have asked before she wrapped up the food.

'No, thank you,' Mma said. She counted out the notes and paid.

Women around here should really learn to mind their own business, she thought as she unwrapped the news-paper and bit into one perfectly fried akara ball. The heat burnt her tongue but she persisted, rolling the food from one cheek to the other. It wasn't even as if her mother had been nice to any of these women! She took another hot bite. She walked up the stairs and unlocked her front door. She banged it behind her. She paced the balcony, eating her food, trying to swallow the anger that had accompanied her all the way from Mama Ekele's. Why did people think that they had a right to question how she chose to bury her own mother? None of the women who passed judgement on her now would let their sons marry her. None of them would let their daughters be friends with her. Yet they wanted to be invited to her mother's burial, to be given presents of food flasks and wall clocks with the deceased's face plastered on them. She walked from one end of the balcony to the other twice, and then went into the sitting room. Sinking into a chair, she spread the news-paper with her food on her lap and began to eat, anger swallowing up her appetite. She did not stop until the food was finished and all that was left was the oil-stained newspaper with the photograph of the state governor, translucent, as if he were a ghost you could see through. Mma did not want to think of ghosts. She rolled up the paper, putting all her energy into the act, as if she were strangling someone. It was only then that she went in and made directly for her mother's bedroom.

She sat on the floor and thought how – even for the time of day – the stillness was unnerving. The otapiapia peddler was probably on holiday too. His 404 pick-up van no longer made the morning rounds, waking up the neighbourhood, singing,

> *Ife na-ata gi si gi n'aka,*
> *o si gi n'aka,*
> *o si gi n'aka,*
> *chinchi na-ata gi si gi n'aka,*
> *onye atana Chukwu uta. Otapiapia!!!*

His voice blaring from the loudspeaker mounted on top of his van: 'Don't blame God for the scourge of pests, any household without otapiapia has only itself to blame. Your destiny is in your own hands.' Mma opened the box.

A marriage like soup is one in a million. The others are just unpalatable concoctions pretending to be soup. Mama Chikezie, I do not know if you remember her – but she and her family lived in the flat where the widower now lives – always had a young female visitor every time her husband was away on a business trip. She said the young woman was a relative but everyone knew that she was more than that. Someone said she spied them once, touching each other like man and woman. Ha! The women can put on their make-up, wear their smiles and put their arms around their husbands when they step out the door but I know that their smiles are fake.

I could fill these pages with stories of our neighbours' 'respectable' marriages but I won't bother. This is my memoir. It is all about me and not about their pretend-pretend relationships.

I want to dwell on happy-happy things. When you were very little we had a game. I am sure you no longer remember. Every morning, you would tell me what you dreamt of the night before. You were not allowed to tell me sad dreams. If you had a sad one, or had forgotten it, you had to make up a nice one. Very often you would tell me you dreamt of me baking you a cupcake, or buying you a bottle of Treetop; or taking you to the park. Once a week, I would fulfil one item on your dream list.

Mma felt tears come to her eyes. Her mother was wrong. She remembered the game, although she had not thought of it before now. How could she have forgotten that she had once been happy? She did not always have to make up a nice dream. The bad dreams were recent. Like the one she had two nights ago.

Her mother had come to her, one half of her face scarred as if she had suffered from chickenpox. She had not said a word but just stood looking at Mma. On her feet were her red shoes, her dancing shoes. Her hands were floppy, as if the bones had been filleted out, and a dusty white, as if they were covered in talcum powder.

59

Mma remembered smelling the choking stench of otapiapia.

She wanted to dance. Dancing helped her forget. She rifled through some cassettes and settled on Madonna. Something quick. Something danceable. Something light. Something to lift the sombreness from her life. She raised the volume and began to twirl and twirl, trying not to think. Not of her mother. Not of the dream. And not of the stories she was uncovering in the shoebox. Her head was bursting and she had to clear it, twirling into forgetfulness. Twirling into a place where the only thing that mattered was Madonna and her happy carefree voice singing, *Holidaay! Celebraate!* The vowels extended to encompass happiness. She danced and danced until she fell exhausted into the chair. She thought of how different her life would be once she married Obi and started to have her own children. She would make healthy food and keep a clean kitchen and find something else to replace otapiapia as her poison of choice. She could not stand its stench. It smelt foul, like death. But surely, some deaths were desirable? She did not need these thoughts crowding her head again. Once she let one come along, another stole in. And another. And another. And another. Until her head felt like it was going to burst and scatter her brains. She put a thumb to the nape of her neck and rubbed. She got up, turned the tape over and started to dance again. This time, though, her movements were slower, as if she had aged. Her bones ached. Her eyes hurt. And the entire house was suffused with that foul, suffocating smell.

She willed her feet to move, faster and faster; she turned up the music until the walls shook and the music entered her body, snaked into her nostrils and covered her tongue, so that there was nothing else but this loud, booming sound and Madonna's voice screaming. She opened her mouth wide, breathing out the words, and sang along and shut her eyes and no longer remembered the beginning of the upside-down thought or the end of it. Because-because. Because it never happened. She danced and danced until her bones turned to liquid.

She had not dreamt of her mother, which was a blessing, but she had dreamt of whiteness. She was in a room filled with white powder, flying above her head. Certain that it was talcum powder, she bent over and scooped up a handful to smear on her face but once she brought it close enough, she recognised that unmistakable smell before it hit her nose fully and engulfed her and brought her down. She woke up sweating with no idea how she had made it to her room. There had been another power outage while she slept and so the fan she usually left on had ceased to blow. It was so hot; she could be moi-moi slowly steamed. She undressed and went into her bathroom for a cold shower. One of the good things about being rich was having enough water to be able to take a shower whatever the time of day. She stood under her shower and, for a while, the only thing she felt was the soothing water running out and cooling her, washing away the smell in her nose and on her tongue.

And then she went back to her mother's room.

7

Mother. Mummy. Music. Mma. *Mamannukwu.* Memories. You can't make the 'M' sound with your nostrils pinched.

She could not breathe with a mother like Ezi. Sometimes, when she was around, Mma felt like she had cotton wool up her nose.

Her restless eyes scanned the neighbourhood and settled on her courtyard, wide and empty like a gaping toothless mouth. Even before the house became hers, she had felt the courtyard belonged to her. She had claimed it from the very beginning. From the moment she was old enough to be hurt, it was hers. It was here she played as a child. And here as a young adult she spent many hours when she needed a break from her mother and her bedroom was not space enough. Its hugeness swallowed her and gave her a sense of freedom. Come January it would be full of playing children, animating the neighbourhood with their shrieks of joy and their howls of distress: the concrete floor was responsible for many grazed knees. She had played there too – hopscotch and *suwe* – and had fallen on its concrete floor and wailed too. She often joked to Obi that ingrained in the floor was the blood of all the children who had lived in the house. Once a child had fallen and broken a tooth but that was the most serious injury anyone ever got, as if the floor itself were human, shielding them from real harm, wanting them to come back and play, secure in the knowledge that they were being looked after. The courtyard had been the set on which so much of her childhood had played out. There, she had experienced the sadness of fighting with her friends and the joy of making up with them, distributing the biscuits and sweets her mother always had in abundance. Her friends had envied her. Their parents thought biscuits and sweets were a waste of money and would never buy any. Now all those girls were gone. All the friends she had played with were gone. They had either moved out with their families or married and left home. None had made any effort to keep in touch.

She had been invited to one wedding – that of her friend Akachi – but the way the invitation card had been wheedled out infuriated Mma so much that she had not turned up. To imagine that Akachi had been one of her closest friends on the courtyard. She had given Mma an invitation on the very week of the wedding itself. And only because Mma had run into her at the market and asked her what she was up to, why had she not been in touch? Would she like to meet up soon? There had been an uncomfortable silence before Akachi announced to her that arranging her wedding kept her too busy for anything else. 'Here is an invitation card. It'd be nice if you could make it.' Mma had wanted to ask her if she would have bothered inviting her had they not bumped into each other, but she hadn't. No need to make things any more uncomfortable, she thought. She had torn up the card as soon as she got home, not even bothering to look at the name of the groom.

She and Akachi had been the best of friends, had they not? She was no longer sure. And what of the other girls with whom she had played and fought? The girls who had happily eaten her sweets and biscuits? What did they think of her? Probably while they were her mother's tenants, they were obliged to be nice to her. And her biscuits and sweets probably added to their willingness. They deferred to her authority as the landlady's daughter. After the run-in with Akachi, her memory of her childhood was never quite the same. She remembered words said, glances exchanged between her friends and their parents which had seemed innocuous enough but which now were weighted with meaning. Their parents cooed them out to play with Mma while keeping a close eye on them from behind their doors to make sure they did not pick up any undesirable behaviour from her. Who knew what lurked in the heart of a wayward woman's daughter? Even a girl with innocent eyes lied. Everyone knew that. They quizzed their children after each play session, wanting to know what Mma said, how she played. Did she touch them? They made their daughters repeat every word of what passed between them and warned them never to enter Mma's house. She held your hand? How?

Just so.

Just so how?

Did she tell you anything?

No.

Nothing at all? Don't lie to me.

64

She just said that I could come in whenever I wanted to watch a film.

Don't you go into that house. Never! If I ever hear that you went, I'll twist your ears until they fall off. You understand?

Yes, Mama. These women were prepared to defer to their landlady but there were limits. Their daughters' morality was at stake. One could never be too careful. Once your reputation was gone, that was it. They could kiss suitable marriages goodbye. And those mothers had plans for their daughters: raise them well and hope a fine young man with a good job snapped them up. They wanted to be mothers-in-law to men who would appreciate the job they had done on their daughters. And if he had money, he would spoil them, too. What was the point of having a daughter if you let another woman spoil her for you?

Mma collected friends outside her neighbourhood, too. Her beauty and her extravagance made her popular, but she hardly kept them. She gathered them and held them close but like the beads of a snapped bracelet, they slipped through her fingers, so that she couldn't retrieve them. It was never long before new friends started to avoid her, to make excuses why they could no longer come to her house, to mumble nervously when she said maybe she could come to their houses instead? Her mother could bring her on Saturday. When their mothers dropped them off they naturally wanted to meet Ezi. They wanted to draw her into conversation and work out the sort of home their daughters were visiting. It was only normal. With sons you could afford to be complacent, but not with daughters. You held your daughters close to your chest, you stifled any desire they might show, you straitjacketed them in sensible brassieres and you kept a close watch on the relationships they formed. These women, their daughters' best interests at heart, asked Mma's mother questions that were sometimes not too subtle. And she, versed in the art of frankness, answered them with no subtlety either.

'So, Mma's father is at work?' they would ask, jangling car keys, smiling nicely, all sweetness.

'No, she has no father. It's just me and her,' she would respond with an open face. No smile. No doubling of her words. No 'father-father' to make her tone less serious.

'Oh, is he late?' The 'late' not inflected as in a question but dropped flatly with certainty. If Mma did not have a father – if the mother could be this casual about that announcement – it must mean that he was dead, poor girl.

'I don't know if he's alive or dead and, frankly, I don't really care. Would you like another glass of water?' Her voice as sharp as a lemon. And the mothers would begin to shift on their chairs as if they were being bitten by ants, their eyes would scan the sitting room, take in its luxury and come to the one logical conclusion. They would uncross their legs, cough and say, 'Actually, my husband needs the car back soon and we'd better start leaving. Thank you for the drink.' And they'd drag their daughters home to safety, and the friendship, just budding, would be nipped. And Mma would be left reeling in despair while her mother laughed and joked that she could hear the women's cars screeching as they sped off to find more suitable playmates for their precious

66

daughters. 'Spawns of the devil,' she would laugh, pinching Mma's cheeks. 'You don't need such friends, my baby-baby. If they don't want you, we don't want them.' She'd seize on an attribute of the just-departed mother and child and ridicule it. 'What a face the mother has! She looks like an ekpo masquerade. What a voice that little girl has. "Twit twit twit." Like a chirruping bird's. What do you need to be friends with such a girl for? Twit-twitting like that all day-day long. And that one walks so ungainly, as if she was being pushed from behind. She doesn't deserve you as a friend, baby-baby. Couldn't wait to be rid of us, the silly idiot!' She laughed but Mma refused to join in.

Even as a child she had mastered the art – without any conscious cunning – of becoming the exact opposite of her mother. Where her mother's laughter was unbridled and loud, Mma's was timid, a chuckle at most. Where her mother's voice was so loud it was not certain whether she was shouting or just plain talking, Mma's voice was low and demure. Her mother sought to see the flaw in everyone, the blemishes, the scars. Mma sought perfection, she saw beauty in everyone. Her mother laughed at the girls who came to see her and Mma was filled with distress, a loathing for her mother who did not seem at all to notice. No. A mother who appeared to delight in her distress. A mother who lived by the rule that men were dispensable. Mma thought them indispensable and was not going to live as her mother lived. Her mother thought she was a fool. 'You fool-fool; men are not worth it.'

Erinne's mother was the only one, of all the mothers, who brought their children to play with Mma, who accepted another drink from Ezi after her revelation of being a single parent. Where others had grabbed their daughters and fled, her response was: 'It must be tough raising a child on your own.'

'Ah, your friend is almost as beautiful as you are, my baby-baby,' Ezi had said later of Erinne.

When Mma became old enough to have friends who did not need to be walked or dropped off by a zealous parent, she was certain her problems were over. Her new friends would judge her on her own merits and not on her mother. It did not take her long to find out just how wrong she was, to discover that zealous parents made zealous young girls who on the cusp of woman-hood were nervous and uptight about the homes their friends came from. Bad homes stank and they did not want to stink. They wanted to attract the right sort of man and the right sort of man did not turn up at Ezi's door. Enugu was too small for girls to be seen in a house of ill repute.

Mma tried not to blame them. She knew they feared what she would become. She was, after all, her mother's daughter. And as everyone knew, prostitution, like crime, was often hereditary. Mma learnt to keep new friends, no matter what they suspected, away from her home. It was safer that way. Once she moved to a new city, she would be able to meet people who knew nothing about her mother, friends who would not judge her based on her history. Her history would be whatever she and Obi decided it would be, she thought. For the first time in her life, she would look people in the eye and say, 'I'm Mma. I'm a respectable young woman.' And there would be no mother lurking in the shadows, waiting to reappear and taint her. She might even join a church. That was the most obvious sign of respectability. She would sing in the choir, be a church warden, show the world her piety, and parents one day would be fighting each other to get their children to be friends with hers. She might even turn Pentecostal, enrol in one of those long-distance Bible School correspondence courses and become a pastor. Pastor Mma! Hmm, definitely had a ring to it. She would have Bible texts at her fingertips, quoting the perfect one for every occasion; parishioners would flock to her with their troubles and she would counsel and guide them to the light. She would be seen as righteous and no one would ever question her morality. Her holiness would bounce off her forehead in flecks of light and people would want to touch her, have her bless them, pray for them. Not a blemish would be found on her, not a single questionable mark.

Her children would never know the truth about their grandmother. No. Not a thing. She would not have her children judging her too. No need for that. She would only tell them that she was beautiful, for that was the only truth she cared to reveal.

Her mother was one of the most beautiful women she had ever seen. In the framed photographs her beauty shone: a not-so-short, not-so-tall woman in platform shoes and a dress that came just to her knees, braids down to her shoulders and a smile revealing white gapped teeth. But not even the smile could hide a hardness around the edges of her mouth. Her complexion is that of freshly, evenly varnished wood. She often said that her nickname was *omuma awu aru*: she who takes a bath just because-because. She was so beautiful she did not need to take baths. She was aware of her own beauty in a way that embarrassed Mma who believed that it was just another sign of her wantonness. Yet Mma was secretly pleased, for there was no denying the fact that the two women were identical, so identical that people often commented on first meeting them that her mother must have simply spat her out. It was this physical similarity which also worried Mma. And so she avoided her mother, and patiently waited for the day she could move out of the house.

Her plan was to become independent as quickly as possible. She had graduated, but getting a job was more difficult than she had anticipated. She had not had the foresight to get a degree in a subject sure to guarantee her a job, but had followed her heart and spent four years studying Theatre Arts. She – unlike many of her classmates – had not even needed to fight her mother for her choice of study. And she was only one of three in her class for whom the course was not a transition into Law or Journalism.

Her graduating class had put on a performance of Wole Soyinka's *Trials of Brother Jero*, and she had won the role of Jero's cantankerous wife, Amope. She had given Amope life that nobody before her had, but even that had not got her a call from the Nollywood directors. She was not greedy, all she wanted was a chance to show how good she could be. A chance to show her mother that she could be independent. Anyone who could perform that well on stage would definitely be able to star in a film. She wondered now if her mother was even aware of her dreams.

8

Mma looked down again at the paper in her hand. It was filled with barely legible writing: tight, terse, scribbles like a child writing in a hurry, the letters rising and falling as if following the patterns of a song, the careful black cursive of the title abandoned. Red ink on white paper. How very typical of her mother, she thought, to write in red. Blue or black would have been too regular, too normal for a woman who once told her daughter she took great pride in living life on her own terms. Once when Mma, at fourteen, went crying to her because a classmate had laughed at her for wearing sandals that were no longer in fashion, she had told her daughter, 'Be a leader, not a follower! No child of mine is going to be a cow. Be the herdsman! Who decides what's fashionable? Who has the right to tell you what's in trend? Your classmates? The media? You are not stylish if you follow the herd. You should stand out. Create your own style, then you'll be truly stylish.' That day, Madam Gold was visiting, and had interceded for Mma. 'Make the girl's life easy, *biko*. Were you not a child yourself once? *Biko*, stop filling her head with leaders and followers, cows and herdsmen, she's not a Fulani nomad,' she scolded Ezi. Turning to Mma, she said, 'Don't mind your mother. If she hasn't bought you

71

a new pair by the time I visit you again, I'll take you myself to Bata and you can choose two pairs of shoes: one for school and one for outings. *I na-egekwa m nti?* Now stop crying. Stop crying! You'll get new shoes before Monday. I promise you that. Now, go and play. Good girl!'

Her mother had seemed slightly piqued but the very next day she had taken Mma to Bata to have her sandals replaced. They even skipped breakfast to beat the traffic. When Madam Gold visited two days later, Mma had shown her the sandals. 'I'm glad your mother saw sense!' Madam Gold said. Ezi had eyed her dramatically. Then they both burst into laughter and started talking about things of which Mma had no understanding. She had often wished at that age that Madam Gold was her mother.

You stood out all right, Mummy, Mma thought, starting to read.

My mother never knew me as a mother. Not really. I have sometimes wondered what she would have made of me had she met you. She never gave me a chance to show her, did she? Not really. I know we have had our problems, you and me, but that is because we are really alike. I can imagine you shaking your head now. But it is true. We are more alike than you care to admit. *Ose na mmanu.* We go together. Think about it, baby-baby, and dare to tell yourself the truth. The truth will set you free!

I wonder who came up with that: the truth will set you free. Nonsense! The truth is many things. It can do many things. But the truth does not

always liberate, does it? It is self-serving and sometimes causes harm. During the war, some people
told the truth of their neighbours hiding grown-up
sons, and got those sons forced into the military,
handed guns and ordered to shoot. The truth has
no hiding place, they say. I say it can stay hidden
and not cause harm. I never wanted the truth! I
could have done without knowing it. Ignorance is
bliss, is it not? There is more truth in that than in
anything we have ever been told about the truth.

There were times I wanted to show you off. To
tell the world: *See what I've done with her!* Did you
know that? I bet you didn't. I know what you
thought of me. I know. But beware, my daughter.
I am not the enemy. The man who refuses to open
his eyes to the excreta his friend has successfully
side-stepped will have no one but himself to blame
when he steps into it. The lizard says that it nods
its head when it falls to encourage itself because
no one else will encourage it. When I think back
on how hard I had to struggle, on what I had to
work with, I too nod my head. I have done a good
job with you, even if you do not realise it.

It was not always easy. You have always been such
a difficult one, baby-baby, but no one can blame
me for not doing my best. Think. Think of all the
good times we had. Remember . . .

Mma hissed and dug into her own memories of growing
up with Ezi. How could she have thought she did a
good job? Her mother had no idea what parenting was!
Taking her to the park and baking her cupcakes, did

73

that qualify her for Mother of the Year? She shut her eyes and inhaled deeply to stop from crying but memories came rushing in.

M. Memories. Beneath all the other memories, the clearest childhood memory Mma had of her mother was of a not-so-tall, not-so-short woman in a multicoloured boubou, clapping and dancing to music Mma could no longer recall. On her feet she had shoes of such glossy red that it seemed as if they sent out sparks every time she tapped them. The boubou billowed around her waist like a parachute and Mma remembered imagining the boubou opening up and sending her mother spiralling upwards into heaven, sparks of fire trailing from her feet. Her mother's face was dominated by a wide, wide smile, as if that was all her face was: a smile that swallowed everything else. It was the smile Mma saw whenever the memory popped into her head. She was there now:

'*Ngwa*, dance, dance,' her mother said to her. And Mma, already embarrassed by her mother's flamboyance (even though it would take her some years to understand why), and irritated by the baby-talk, shook her head. She was quite upset with her mother.

'No-no? Come, sweetie, come dance-dance with your mummy-mummy,' her mother said, the smile never diminishing. She reached out to drag Mma up from the sofa but Mma sank deeper into it, as if wanting to meld herself to the velvet cushions.

'Get up, get up and dance-dance with Mummy-Mummy.'

Mma said, 'No.' She did not want to dance. She sat on the sofa with her doll in one hand, like trying to behave herself at someone else's house. She felt like a stranger. Her mother scolded her once: 'You lurk-lurk in corners as if you were only visiting-visiting.'

Her mother turned her back to her now, bunched up her boubou in one hand so that her thighs showed, wriggled her buttocks, threw a leg up and brought it down as if it were a tree she were planting, reconnecting it to the earth. Mma was convinced that her mother was so solid that nothing could remove her, not even death.

She remembered that day so well.

Ogochukwu-from-downstairs' mamannukwu was visiting, and had come like Father Christmas, bearing sacks of gifts: fruit; gold-coloured cocoa and dark violet pears; green guavas the size of a human fist and sour-sop with green bumpy skin like a baby dinosaur. Mma wanted her own grandmother to visit too. She wanted this, perhaps, more than she had ever wanted anything else at that age.

'When is my mamannukwu visiting?'

'It's just the two of us, baby-baby,' her mother replied, interrupting her dance to give her daughter a quick hug. 'Just baby-baby and her mummy-mummy. No mamannukwu.'

Mma would not give up. She wriggled out of her mother's hug. 'But where is my mamannukwu?' Surely, everyone had one tucked away in the countryside. Mma was not sure where exactly. She had lived in Enugu all her life, and did not, like the other children she knew, take regular trips 'home' with her mother. But that was a minor point. Like buttocks, every child had to have a pair of what Mma was becoming convinced was essential to their happiness: a village and a grandmother in that village. All the other children spoke of their grand-mothers, whether they visited often or not, but Ogochukwu-from-downstairs had become unbearable since her grandmother came from Ezinifite. These days, she started every sentence with, 'Mamannukwu m said' and 'Mamannukwu m did'. Her mamannukwu told her stories every night. Sometimes Ogochukwu was generous and shared them with her friends, but always she would let them know that she was, like an impolite host saving the choicest bits of meat for himself, saving the best stories for herself. When they begged her for more, she said, 'My mamannukwu says if she piled up all the stories she knows, eh, they would fill this entire compound!' And then she would give a quick smile and ask, 'Did you like my story?'

'Yes!' They had laughed so hard when Tortoise lost all the feathers he had borrowed and was thrown down from the skies. They hoped their scream was enough to guarantee another tale.

'You think this story is great? Hmm, the one she told me two nights ago was better,' Ogochukwu said, laughing as they begged her to relent.

'Please tell us, *biko nu*.'

'No. That story is for me. Do you think stories grow on trees? You think you can just go and pluck them for nothing?'

Tired of begging, one of the children said, 'Wait till my mamannukwu comes. She will tell me better stories than yours. Your grandmother is a rubbish storyteller who waddles like a duck with three feet and smells like a village latrine.'

'And your grandmother is a witch with hair on her chin and no teeth. She has a dirty mouth like you. I am never sharing my mamannuwku's cocoa and stories with you again!'

Mma did not care if the woman waddled like a duck or was toothless (of course, it would be better if she came perfect and did not smell: Ogochukwu-from-downstairs' mamannukwu did have a certain odour to her), as long as she was able to say *Mamannukwu m said . . .* and told stories and came with sacks of cocoa and huge delicious guavas, the size of which could never be found in Enugu.

Mma's mother kept dancing, the red shoes sinking their heels into the rug, sparkling as she moved, failing to grasp her daughter's need. It was this failure (how could she smile and dance away while her daughter suffered?) which got Mma upset. How old had she been then?

'Come dance-dance with Mummy-Mummy.'

And Mma had refused and sought solace in her doll, burying her head in its stringy hair. Breathing in its doll-scented smell. Ah, where was that doll now? She had no memory of losing it. It just seemed like it was there one day and, unnoticed, had slipped away the next. Like so many things in her life.

But Mma did have a grandmother. She did have a mamannukwu who could have visited and who she could have shown off. And like everything else, her mother had kept her existence hidden. And she dared to think that she had done a good job? 'No, Mummy, you didn't!' Mma screamed into the room. 'No amount of cupcakes, of picnics, of bottles of squash will ever make up for your meanness to me!'

What if she had refused to read those letters? She had never meant to read them after all. Her grandmother would have been removed from her history. What sort of a woman does that to her own daughter? But what sort of a daughter, she caught herself thinking, was she? Madam Gold had asked her the very same question on the day Ezi died.

9

Mma got off the floor and sat on the bed, settling the shoebox beside her. She wiped her eyes with the back of one hand and sniffed. Her nose was running and she wiped it with the edge of the bed sheet. At the back of her head, she could hear a sound like the muffled hum of distant cars. She lay down and clapped her hands over her ears.

Some things were not worth remembering. Why did her mother choose to set some memories down and not others? And the ones she did not set down – deliberately or out of forgetfulness – Mma would never know of. She did not want to think of the history she did not know of, because the one her mother was revealing was already too much to bear. Even though it was hot, she was shivering. She pulled the bed sheet over her and all the way up to her chin. The shivering would not stop. The muffled hum became louder and screamed into the room and silenced it. Mma sat up on the bed and held her head in her hands. She felt overwhelmed by a sudden sense of tedium. She asked herself why she persisted in reading if all it did was weigh her down, drag her into this dark pit where she heard noises in her head and shivered in the heat. Perhaps her mother was right, and the truth is not always liberating. Perhaps, she thought, this was her mother's own self-indulgent joke: leave her daughter a memento that is sure to hurt her. She had spent the past hour reading about shiny cars and lovers. She picked up the letters.

Enugu wasn't a place where you could hide a secret. Especially not if the secret were a living breathing thing. And not if you lived in a block of flats where everything was shared: kitchen, bathroom, toilet, personal business. When they asked you personal questions, you couldn't complain because if you did, you were told that you should have married a rich man who had enough money to buy you a duplex in Independence Layout or GRA, where people lived in isolation like Europeans and everyone minded their own business and where a young woman with a child and no wedding ring on her finger could move in and did not invite rumours. But if you were that young woman and you moved to a flat in Uwani you left yourself open to rumours.

Ah! The things that were said about me! Did I answer them? Did I stoop to their level to dispel the rumours? My silence was seen as proof of guilt and the rumours were fed daily and gained so much weight they became obese. If I had let them, those stories would have crushed me. I remained jolly-jolly. This annoyed the neighbourhood. A woman who was accused of the things they said I did ought to have shown some shame. She should have shouted her innocence. She should have demurely deferred to the moral superiority of the others and walked with downcast eyes. I was their Hester Prynne. They were furious with me. When they asked about my husband, they expected that I would seek their pity and say he was dead, even though I had no wedding band on. They would have forgiven me the lie because it meant I sought their approval at least. I refused to acknowledge my wrongs by not telling a lie. I told them I had no husband. When they raised their eyebrows and asked about the father of my baby, I told them you had no father. You should have seen their faces! It was a reckless thing to say in a city whose dashing young governor was reputed to have an eye for the ladies and women became rich overnight by sleeping with the cabinet. And I was beautiful enough to catch the eye of any governor on any given day. If I was sleeping with the governor, did they think I would choose to live in that cramped one-room flat? I did not even have my own bathroom!

The women snubbed me and, when their husbands tried to catch my eye and I ignored them, they joined their wives to mutter, 'Who does this woman think she is? She and her bastard child. She's nothing but a prostitute!' How those men could have thought I wanted anything to do with them. I wanted a better life for myself and my baby, not someone else's husband who was struggling himself to make ends meet. Someone dragging-dragging me down. And for what?

When they noticed the cars that came to pick me up – Mercedes Benzes and BMWs with shiny wheel covers – the rumours gained more strength and pushed us both away from the rest of the neighbourhood. It marked me – and by extension you, too – as someone to be avoided. Women refused to babysit you, my beautiful baby-baby. You were the most beautiful child that neighbourhood had ever seen, yet when you cried, nobody offered to hold you and try to console you like they did with each other's babies. Nobody said, 'Bring that crying baby here, *nwa bu nwa ora*. She belongs to all of us.' Nobody asked to carry you, or sang of how beautiful you were or let you suckle on their dried-out nipples in consolation. The women forbade their husbands from fixing things around our house and so one evening when my electricity tripped, even though Papa John from upstairs was an electrician of some repute, and regularly helped out the other tenants, I had to strap you to my back and go in search of one from outside the neighbourhood. I missed my friends from Kaduna. I missed my life, baby-baby, and I tried very hard not to. I was jolly-jolly but inside me I was shaking-shaking. One day I . . . No, better not to write that. No need going over that soil now. It is no longer fertile.

'She has roving eyes,' the women said of me, and no man was safe, least of all theirs. Some of them called me Jezebel to my face. They called me Daughter of Satan, and said loudly to each other that they had to protect their families from me. Papa John's wife told me one day that my eyes were fire waiting to consume her husband. 'Don't you see how they shine? Those eyes!' Did I answer her? Your mummy-mummy said nothing. I have a mouth on me now but in those days I didn't. I should have told her that I had no use for a man as short as her husband. Oh! And his head was shaped like an egg. If it were now, I would have told her that her husband was so ugly I would not even spit on him!

The women guarded their men with watchful eyes and sharp-sharp tongues. Whereas you and I had attracted curiosity initially, now we were treated like people who had become contagious, as though we had just escaped from the leper colony in Oji River and come to taint them all. Ah! They made me wish I truly was one of the governor's mistresses. I'd have asked him to lend me some policemen just to harass their stupid lives.

The owners of the cars themselves did not come, they sent their drivers: lanky men with unfashionable haircuts and amused looks who came knocking on my door so loudly that all the neighbours heard. Of course, I knew they did it on purpose to humiliate me, the reason for their working at a time when they could have been napping or sleeping with their own women or running around doing their own business. I would scurry out in my miniskirt and high, high heels, you in my arms, and be driven away while neighbours watched from behind their curtains and speculated in loud voices where I was being taken to. I could imagine what they asked each other. I could imagine their laughter, loud and wild, accompanied by much slapping of thighs. On the rare occasions when the big men

83

came themselves, they did not get out of their cars but beeped their horns to bring me out, much to the anger of the neighbours, who asked in loud voices if their compound was too dirty for the big men to come in and collect their whore, and were they not ashamed of themselves? Had they no wives to go home to? And did they know all the things they could catch from a woman like me? Stupid women. They should come and see me now!

It was not very practical carrying you around and so I had to get a maid. A little girl who babysat you while I stayed out late at night. Neighbours said it was obvious now, I was definitely a prostitute. When I queued up outside the compound to fetch water from the tap, they shouted, 'Whore!' '*Ashawo!*' 'Shameless woman.' If they bumped into me in the kitchen or the bathroom, they hissed loudly and held their noses as if I smelt. They waylaid my maid whenever she was outside and asked her what she was doing with me, had she no family who cared for her? It was better, they told her, for her family to live in poverty than to hire out to such a woman who would surely corrupt her soul. What was the world coming to, they asked, when families sent out little girls to live with whores?

Determination makes one impervious to pain. I ignored the women. But one night I came home to find my window broken and a drunken neighbour singing outside my door, saying that he too could 'service a lonely young woman', his sugarcane was as sweet as any rich man's. And no one, not a single neighbour, came to my rescue. It did not matter that there was a baby in the house with a young girl. I knew then that nobody there would help. They would hand out stones with which to pelt me.

S is for silly. S is for stupid. If you pull it long enough, it becomes a furious hiss. 'You were a stupid, stupid woman!' Mma shouted, barely containing the urge to throw something at the wall. 'You were a stupid woman and I hate you! I hate you!' Something painful settled in her chest and she took deep breaths to keep from bursting into a wail. She looked at her watch. The hour she had given herself was not yet up. She groaned but kept on.

Whereas the snide remarks by the neighbours had not got to me, this attack shook me to the bone. I resolved to accept an offer that I had been rejecting. I had my beautiful baby-baby to think of, after all. The next day, I left. The maid would not come with me. Papa John's wife had ferreted out her parents' address from her and sent word to them to come and rescue their daughter from the devil's lair. Sure, they needed the wages she was paid but not at that price. What were the chances of their daughter finding a husband once it was known what sort of a woman she lived with? There were many families in a city like Enugu looking for maids. Decent families. Their daughter would not be unemployed for long. Half of the women in that compound wanted her for themselves. The girl was a hard worker!

On a Saturday morning I tucked you under one arm, my suitcase under the other, hailed a cab and did not look back at the crowd of neighbours that had gathered. I pretended not to hear their boos and laughter. Instead, I waved from my seat, the way I imagined the Queen of England did when she was being driven around the city and crowds of worshipping subjects gathered to catch a glimpse of her. A slow movement of one hand, a firm smile on my lips aimed at no one and my thoughts already occupied with other things. This house on Neni Street for one.

10

Neni Street was a gift from a married man who always swore that had he been Muslim he would have married Ezi and raised Mma as his very own. Ezi assured him that it would not have mattered because she had never wanted to be a second wife, their relationship suited her just fine the way it was. He had given the house to her so that it could become their love nest. He did not like sneaking into hotels for a few hours of good-time, he was too big for that and she was too good for it. It would diminish what they had. Besides, he did not like the idea of ordering room service when they got hungry after sex. Here there was a kitchen so that Ezi could cook while he played with Mma and fantasised about living like that for the rest of his life. The flat they occupied had enough rooms. One room for him and Ezi when he visited and another room for Mma and her nanny when she got one. But the house had been given to her on one condition: Ezi had to be exclusively his. No man, no matter how platonic his relationship with Ezi, was allowed to visit her. For a while she had resisted. She liked the freedom that came with not being anyone's. Madam Gold – who by now was back in her life – was instrumental in getting her to change her mind. Perhaps it was not a bad thing,

Madam Gold told her, for Mma to have a stable father figure in her life. And Madam Gold had always had her ear.

Mma remembered the man. He walked around the house, shirtless, a wrapper tied around his waist, the way fathers did. For a long time Mma thought he was her father, even though she never called him Daddy. He pinched her cheeks and gave her presents of sweets and colouring books. He sometimes sat with her while she coloured, dutifully complimenting her on how well she worked. He lifted her on to his shoulders and played with her and called her Little Madam. The only times she did not like him was when he spent the night and she was banned from her mother's room. Even the extra presents she was plied with on such nights did not compensate for the loss of her place beside her mother in her bed. In the morning, they would tease Mma about her sulking, tell her pouting would age her quickly, and give her an extra egg at breakfast. He would tickle her and make her laugh so that her world became balanced again, and she would forget she was angry with him.

At some point while she was growing up, he vanished from their lives. She had missed him for a while, had asked her mother when he would be coming back to visit, but her mother never gave any response, letting the silence swell until Mma could no longer stand it and left the room. When she answered at all, it was to tell Mma not to interfere in grown-up affairs. Children should be busy-busy with their play-play. Mma knew better than to argue and so she kept her disappointment to herself. She remembered walking around for days feeling as if her heart had a hole that was sifting sand, waiting for the man she wished was her father to turn up at their doorstep. He never did. And no other man came to replace him. She wondered what happened to him.

Mma began to get curious about her father when she started primary school. Her schoolmates talked about their fathers and what they did. For Show and Tell in class one, Mmeri brought in a baton, and talked about her father, the policeman: 'The best policeman in the whole wide world. With this baton, he chases thieves and clubs them over the head: bam, bam, bam!' She brandished the baton above her head. Mmeri's story had impressed everyone and they had listened wide-eyed as she talked of her father's exploits and how he was not scared of any bandit, not even the feared Anini. 'My daddy says if he catches him, he will club him over the head, one blow for every highway robbery he has done, and he will never ever steal again!'

Everybody had clapped for her and for her fearless policeman father. And when it was Mma's turn, she had spoken about her doll which she named Amaka, with the plastic face and long shiny hair. The applause for her was muted. Dolls were not very interesting for Show and Tell unless they were dolls that could walk and talk like Amelia's, which her father had brought her from London. Mma could not talk about a father she knew nothing about.

Even those whose fathers were dead knew who they were or what they had been; they had memories or their mothers' memories, they talked about their fathers with affection in their voice, which made Mma envious and filled her with longing.

When Mma asked her mother who her father was, her mother's response was always, 'You do not have a father.' Her voice, bored, as if she would rather be talking about something else. But you could not tell your classmates, 'My mummy says I don't have a daddy.' What sort of a response was that? So Mma put her fantasies into words and spun elaborate stories for her curious classmates of a father with a long beard who could spin a football on his index finger, but who had died in a car crash when she was five years old.

She hated her mother for not trying to create a story for her or answering when asked by a daring classmate why there were no photos of the deceased father on the sitting-room walls.

'In my house,' one of the classmates, Binachi, said, 'my daddy's picture has a garland around it so that everyone knows that he is dead. When I am naughty, my mummy talks to the picture. She says that my daddy can hear her from heaven. He is an angel now and has wings.' In drawing class, Binachi drew her father with wings and called him Angel Daddy.

Mma was young, but she was not blind. When she was old enough to realise that her mother had male guests but hardly any female ones, she could guess what her mother did. Now, sitting on her bed and reading about men who visited in cars and of a lover's gift of a house, she felt bile rise in her throat. Why did her mother think she wanted confirmation?

Ezi could rent out the two flats under theirs and she did. With the money she saved she bought other properties in the city: one in New Haven and two duplexes in Trans Ekulu, where rents were high and rising, attracting bank workers and expatriate workers from Emenite who were never behind on their rent and who treated the properties with respect. When one of her tenants returned to his country, he left shiny new pots and pans in the kitchen. Ezi brought the pans home. The plot on New Haven was not yet built. When it was newly acquired, her mother had dreamt of putting up a sprawling bungalow with a swimming pool. 'Pool-pool in my backyard,' she told Mma. It did not matter that she could not swim, it was the statement she was interested in. 'All the good houses have swimming pools. I want one shaped like an egg.' She had cut out pictures of houses from the interior design magazine *You and Your Home*, making a collage of the sort of house she wanted. She would have terrazzo floors in the kitchen with an American fridge that served crushed ice at the press of a button and pissed water from a tiny hole. 'Ha! Water-water from a hole, piss me water from a hole,' she sang, causing Mma to roll her eyes.

All three bedrooms would have en-suite bathrooms with bidets (perfect for soaking stained underwear overnight) and shiny chrome taps. ('Shiny-shiny so I can see my face in it.') She would have a study with a fireplace for the cold harmattan nights. ('Yes,' Mma heard her tell Madam Gold, 'I know that I do not need a fireplace but I can roast ube and corn in the fire.') On the outside, the house would be ringed by four columns. People would stop outside the gate just to admire it. Let me see then if anyone would dare cast aspersions on the type of person to live in that kind of house! And then that high, grating laugh. This was her one big project, her one big dream, the bungalow with an egg-shaped swimming pool in New Haven with bidets for doing the washing in. ('Yes, I know what it is for, Mma, but if it's in my house, I shall dictate its use. People have done laundry in worse places!')

There was no way Mma would be fulfilling her mother's dream, no way she would run the risk of making Ezi happy in death. Let her suffer in the afterlife. It was said that when people died with plans unfulfilled, their spirits roamed the earth and did not find rest until someone brought those plans to fruition. Well, her mother could roam the earth until her feet got sore and her toes gangrened and her heels calloused, Mma simply did not care.

She had thought of selling the plot. It was in a prime area and she was sure to get good money for it. She had also toyed with the idea of donating it to charity just to rile her mother's spirit. She knew how strong her mother's aversion to charity was. Donating it would be the surest way to torture her mother's spirit, to keep her not only restless but angry. The thought of it tickled her. Giving away her mother's most prized possession to charity. This was, after all, a woman who told an eight-year-old Mma that the poor were often very wily, when Mma asked why she never dropped coins in the bowls of beggars who rushed to cars in traffic jams and rapped on windows chanting, '*Abeg*, madam, *abeg sah*, just small money for chop-chop. I never chop since two days.' Her mother barely even looked at them, keeping her face set on the slow-moving traffic ahead. And when she did (especially if they were young women or young girls), it was to tell them that she knew their sort. 'Get out of my sight! *Ndi oshi*,' she would hiss. 'They are thieves, *ndi oshi*. Every single one of them. Never trust the poor.'

'What sort of a person treats the poor this way?' Mma had once asked.

'The sort that has been bitten by the poor,' her mother responded. But Mma herself could not think of a single charity she trusted. The kind of stories she heard tried her willingness to believe in altruistic motives. Everyone wanted to make money. She was probably better off selling the land and banking the money. But she was not in a hurry to plot her revenge. She had time to think about what she would do. She was not strapped for cash. In fact, she had more money than she would ever need. She tried not to feel grateful to her mother for the inheritance. After everything her mother put her through, setting her up for life was the least she owed her. It was only fair. Even Obi told her that. When she said how uncomfortable it made her to benefit from her mother's lifestyle, Obi had said, 'Don't be silly. That woman ruined your childhood. Could she ever compensate enough for that?'

11

L is for love. It's lifting the tongue and placing it gently against the roof of your mouth. L is gentle, like softly saying, *la la la*. It is fluffy like love. Love is patient and kind. Love is not envious or boastful. Love is not forward and self-assertive, nor boastful and conceited. Mma could still quote the passage she had learnt from the Book of Corinthians for her Bible Studies examination many years ago. She imagined love as a beautiful butterfly flitting around a room, sure of itself.

Love was not at all like her mother. That her mother could have loved was a revelation to her. When on the third day of reading the letters, she read about her mother falling for a man, she clapped her hands and said into the room, '*Na wah!* My own mother in love?'

Growing up she always thought of her mother as immune to love, even to that of her daughter. She did not walk around the house singing *la la la*. She sang songs that were heavy on the tongue, and she sang them in a deep, gravelly voice, as if she were a heavy smoker. She opened her mouth wide and she dredged them out like she would a dry cough. Love was not something Mma would ever have associated with the woman who told her that the only criterion she should have for marrying a man was that he had enough money to keep her in the style in which she had been raised. 'Love disappoints,' she said to Mma several times. 'He who trusts in love is a big fool.' Although neither woman was ever able to have a conversation around the minutiae of daily life, Ezi had been adept at churning out cynical homemade aphorisms that irritated Mma. Ezi scoffed at love. 'Love-love nonsense never does anyone any good.'

On the two occasions when Mma had her heart broken by men – men who had promised to marry her but had baulked at the last minute – Ezi had refused to console her, even though she must have known that she was the reason for each man's change of heart. Instead she cautioned her. 'That's what you get for loving. Next time, try using your head. Look out for number one. Look out for a man who'd take you as you are.'

Mma had told Erinne, 'If my mother could, she would pick up the shards of my shattered life and cut me with them. She delights in inflicting pain!'

And so, having read of lovers who drove shiny cars and gave practical gifts, the last thing Mma expected to read about was a man whom her mother had loved-loved with all her heart.

When I met Mike, I was twenty-two. It is hard to believe that I was once that young. The older one gets, the more difficult it is to imagine that one was ever very young. Mike was twenty-seven and swore to make me his wife before the year ran out. His confidence was attractive. He was a handsome man. Very handsome. Very dandy. He always had a scarf knotted around his neck like a film star. The first time I saw him, I thought he looked very much like one of the Jackson 5, Jackie. They had the same lean face and their afros were roughly of the same height. I told him this, and I think it pleased him. In those days, every young man wanted to look like the Jacksons. I was very flattered that he noticed me and even more so that he liked me.

When Mike took me on the long trip home to meet his mother, I was nervous. I was almost sick-sick in the car from wondering if she would like me, and what would happen if she did not. I should not have worried. You know sometimes you meet people and you connect so well, it is as though you reincarnated from the source? So it was with us. We took to each other instantly. She spread her hands and I walked into a tight embrace. My body held the memory of that hug for a very long time. She could not stop paying me compliments. 'You are a very beautiful girl!' 'You are a very modest girl!' 'You are a good-natured girl!' On and on it went the entire day. I did not eat like a greedy girl. I did not drink like a wayward girl. I did not sit like a bad girl. I could do no wrong. Mike thought it auspicious and told me that it was certainly a sign that I was the one for him, he could stop looking for his soul mate.

All around the country, people glowed with the prosperity of the recent Udoji Award. President Gowon had increased the minimum wage of civil servants by more than a hundred per cent and people laughed for no reason at all, as if they had been infected by a happiness bug. But for Mike, that happiness, those smiling faces, were especially for him, for the luck he had had in finding a woman who was not only acceptable to him, but acceptable to his mother as well, he said.

'We've met in the spirit,' his mother told me before we had been in the house an hour. 'I'm glad he's found you. And with those child-bearing hips of yours, you'll soon be filling up the house with babies! You don't want to hear about some of the women he's brought here, hoping for my blessing. *Ndi agahara*, girls whose eyes were up, up, up there in the clouds, they could never make good wives for anyone. I see me in you. Any man would be proud to marry you.'

Who would not be flattered to hear her future mother-in-law talk of her like that? I think I spent all of that day giggling, feeling very grateful to this plump woman with huge eyes who took me in with so much warmth. Maybe I should have worried that her compliments were excessive, but I did not think them so then. People who are quick to pay compliments, baby-baby, are also quick to withdraw them. But wisdom comes with age. She could not praise me enough. She told Mike to hurry up and pay my bride price to ensure that I did not escape him. 'Girls like her are very rare, Mike. Don't let what's yours become someone else's!' I grinned.

Mike complained later that I had spent more time with his mother on that visit than I had with him. Who was I getting married to? It was a mock complaint. You could see from the glint in his eyes that he was proud of this. That his mother who, on their father's death, had grown very possessive of Mike and his older brother Egbuna, who had found faults with every woman Mike had brought home, was totally besotted with me. This was a marriage that was fated to be. I imagined all the grandchildren I would gift to his mother.

His mother showed me the baby pictures of Mike, and I imagined having children who would look like him. His mother told me, 'He was a beautiful baby. Gave me no trouble at all. He hardly cried, not even when he was cutting his first tooth. Your children will be the same.' I smiled at that and said 'Amen' to seal the woman's wish and make it a prayer. Amen. Amen. Amen. A hundred times over.

She asked me to sit in the kitchen with her while she taught me how to make Mike's favourite dishes, revealing the secret of her breadfruit porridge that he said outclassed even the one served in the Ukwa Express, reputed to serve the most delicious breadfruit porridge in the East Central State. She showed me the right amount of akanwu to use and when to add that dash of palm oil that makes all the difference.

It was she who told me that Mike preferred his egusi with achi. 'Not too much, otherwise its taste will overpower that of the egusi.' And as she chopped up bitter leaf to add to the pot, she caught the look on my face and said, 'He likes his egusi not with pumpkin leaves, but with bitter leaf. Yes, strange, but his father did too. At home we would never use bitter leaf. I kept my husband loyal to me by learning his tastes and adapting my cooking to them. Do the same with Mike and he'll never wander!'

I smiled through the lessons and stored them away to use on my husband. And when the old woman whispered, 'Anything you want him to stop, any bad habit, this is the time to get him to stop it. Once you are married, he'll not be too eager to give in to you any more,' I was sure that she and I would be friends for life. I thanked her for the piece of advice. And what a blessing it was, I thought, to have my mother-in-law on my side.

My own mother always told me that in every marriage there are three people: the husband, the wife and the man's mother. 'Sons are tied to their mothers,' she had warned me when I told her we were going to visit Mike's mother. 'Endear yourself to her, call her "Mama" even before she invites you to do so. Make her love you and your marriage will never have any problems. Show an interest in her when you get there. If you don't like her, pretend.' I thought how lucky I was that we had taken to each other so quickly and so naturally: there was no need for tiresome pretence.

'Come back and visit me again soon' she told me when we left.

I began to visit her on my own, using a trip to my parents as the excuse for travelling down to the east. I let the woman fill my ears with stories of Mike's childhood, helping me to piece together a history of the man I loved. I learnt that he had not walked until he was almost two years old. 'We thought he was lame!' his mother said.

On another visit, I heard of how once in a fight with Egbuna, Egbuna had poured the water used for washing sliced yam on Mike. 'He ran around that day like a mad man, scratching and screaming that he was dying, and how could Egbuna have poured that on him? He has a good heart. He is not very good at being cruel to others.'

Sometimes I did not tell Mike where it was I was going to because I did not want to appear too eager to marry him, to insinuate myself into his family and so scare him off. Everybody knows it: if a girl makes herself too easy a catch, men lose interest immediately. The games we play, baby-baby, why?

Mike's mother could not have been prouder than mine at our wedding later that year. She danced. She sang. She ululated. She told anyone who would listen that I was the best gift Mike had ever given her. She cried that her husband was not alive to share the happy day. My mother cried with joy to see me so accepted. Her own mother-in-law had been a proverbial one. Nothing she did was ever good enough for my father's mother. 'If I cooked, it was always too salty or not salty enough.'

I smiled-smiled throughout the day. In all the wedding photographs, my smile was natural and easy. A husband I loved-loved and a mother-in-law who adored me. What could go wrong?

Mma could imagine the dashing young man courting her mother. The thought made her smile. It made her feel tender and gave her the impossible desire to be flung back to those days before she was born. To see how her mother was then as a girl, to see the man who would become her father.

On that day, the third after discovering the letters, when she was at Madam Gold's, she had asked her, 'If my grandmother loved my mother, and my father loved her, why did she leave then?'

'Your grandmother loved your mother at the beginning,' Madam Gold had said. 'Your father used to joke that if he had not married her, his mother would have castrated him. That's how much she wanted the marriage. Your mother was a catch!' She dipped her hand into her brassiere and brought out her handkerchief, wiping sweat off her forehead. She tucked it back into the middle of her bra where it formed a little ball underneath her blouse.

'Not every daughter-in-law got on as well with her mother-in-law as your mother did with hers. She felt particularly grateful for this. She had an ally in this woman, should she ever need one. But Mike treated her like a jewel. "*Ola m*, you are my jewel," he told her often. And she had believed him. And went on believing him through many years of marriage and the trials that came with them. All marriages had their fair share of trials – true – but theirs were worse than any of her friends'. She believed in him through all of that. How he had supported her when his mother turned. Who would have thought it? The woman asking her to release her son with whatever juju she used in binding him! E would have forgiven him anything, anything at all to pay him back for all the many years of support in the face of his family's displeasure – as if all that happened were her fault. As if they did not know that if anything was wrong, it was as much their son's fault as it was hers – but nothing could persuade her to forgive him for Rapu. And he who knew her better than anyone else should have been able to foresee that. He should have been able to predict what her reaction would be. E was not like the rest of us. We . . . we are more pliable.

'The problem is that those with buttocks do not know how to sit,' Madam Gold declared firmly.

When on that day, after the discovery of a father, Mma had gone to Madam Gold and had discovered also a grandfather, she returned with not one address but two scribbled on a sheet of paper, and she had no doubt that she would go in search of both men. In search of the life that should have been hers. The waiting had only made her impatient.

12

M is for mamannukwu. Mamannukwu sounds like a long note of music drenched in honey. Mamannukwu. Syrupy brown face. Her mother's mother. The love was instantaneous. It filled her up. She could not help it. She took in the face. A face filling a huge picture frame, the way pictures of the deceased displayed at wake keepings usually are. Madam Gold had that done for Ezi, too, even though there was no one to gather in front of the huge photograph and mourn in loud broken voices. 'Oh, Ezi, why have you left us? What will we do without you? *Chei!* Death has done its worst. It has carried away the best of us. *Onwu*, ooo! Shame on you, death. Shame on you.'

Mma had often wondered where that tradition had come from, blowing up faces and framing them. Perhaps it sought to defy death by making the deceased larger than life. She had always found it ridiculous, but now she was glad of it, grateful that it gave her a chance to see clearly the grandmother she had never known. Her wrinkles looked so real that Mma was tempted to reach out and touch them. She imagined the warmth of this woman's hands. The stories she would have told her granddaughter. 'Ah, when your mother was a baby, she did this and that.' 'Ah, you are the spitting image of your mother at the exact same age.' She would have shown her grandmother off, be spoilt by her. Ogochukwu-from-downstairs would never ever have laughed at her for the lack of a grandmother. She rubbed a palm against the glass of the frame which held the picture as if she were wiping it of dust. She could feel the tears gather in her eyes but the last thing she wanted to do was to cry here. She closed her eyes and opened them when she knew the tears had retreated. She looked at the photograph again.

The woman was smiling. Mma recognised the open teeth which her mother had. Ezi had told her that it was a sign of beauty, and that in the old days, many women went to roadside carpenters to chip off their teeth. Mma did not know whether she was joking or not. 'Chip-chip,' Ezi laughed. 'But I was born with it. Blessed by nature with it!' She never mentioned that she had inherited it from her own mother. There was a deep dimple in one cheek. Her eyes, rimmed with black eye-pencil, looked startled. Mma recognised that look. Her mother had it too. Young eyes. Even with the crow's-feet, their youthful intensity remained.

Her grandfather noticed her looking at the photo-graph and said, 'Your mother was the image of your grandmother. You remind me of her too. Your eyes are shaped exactly the same.'

Mma ran a finger around one eye, as if realising just at that moment that she was in possession of them.

'So much time. So much time. Your mother was an impatient woman.' He smiled sadly to reveal yellowed teeth. 'I remember when she was small, this small . . .' He indicated a height somewhere around his upper thigh. 'She burnt her tongue because she could not wait for her soup to cool down. She was born impatient!'

Mma had never thought of her mother as a child. But of course she must have been a child once, like everyone else, she thought, smiling at the idea.

'In church, she would spend so much time fidgeting, wanting to know how much longer we had before we went home. Her legs were always itching to move. She could never sit still. But she was very intelligent. *O ma akwukwo rinne.* Her teachers liked her a lot. Good report cards, every term. Her principal had wanted her to go into nursing or teaching. Respectable professions for women. But your mother refused. She had her own plans, she said. She was bent on going to the university, succeeding in a man's world. Did you know that she once swore to your grandmother that she would never get married?' Her grandfather chuckled – a dry, rough sound like a cough. 'We were relieved when she met your father. When she could not conceive we worried that he would kick her out. And then when she had you—' He broke off and coughed. When he coughed, he did not open his mouth wide and cup a hand over his mouth like most people would. Instead he clenched his teeth as if to stop the cough from escaping and spread his lips as if in a smile. For a minute Mma thought he was chuckling. 'We missed her.' There was a long silence. Mma remembered how, as a child, she liked drinking water immediately after she had had a mint because of the sensation of coldness it produced. She looked around the room, very much a man's room. There was a small fridge by the window. It let out intermittent groans. In front, an old shirt soaked up the water it leaked. She remembered how she used to scrape the freezer of ice to plop into her mouth, much to her mother's anger. 'Adamma! You'll spoil the fridge if you keep on doing that!' Mma could not stop. Every opportunity she got, she used, often moulding the ice and filling a cup with it to enjoy in the privacy of her room. Even now, she wanted to claw her fingers into the freezer compartment. She looked away from the fridge and for a while her eyes settled on the window. It was covered with a green mosquito net, discoloured by sun and dust. Her mother used to beat the dust out of their mosquito nets once a week, releasing the trapped dust into the house. Mma always complained.

The bed they sat on was sturdy but low. Beside the fridge stood an office desk with a leatherbound Bible on it and a basket of fruit: one huge pawpaw, some guava and two ripening mangoes. Behind the fruit basket, against the wall, was a transistor radio with a broken aerial. A muffled whining emerged. On the bedside table was an open tub of shea butter, and she caught a whiff of it; but the overwhelming smell in the room was of very strong mentholated balm. She could even feel it stinging her eyes.

'How did she go?' her grandfather asked finally.

Mma could not think of the death. If she did, the smell of otapiapia would come back and she would have to run outside. She did not often think of her mother's burial. It had seemed surreal. Mma's papannukwu was a slight man. He had the stature and the height of a young boy. His skin was dry and papery, like a leaf in the dry season, and she had the curious thought that if she touched it, it would crackle and disintegrate beneath her fingers. Maybe she had inherited her dry skin from him, she thought. His face was lined with wrinkles, deep grooves that seemed so settled they could have been there since the beginning of time. But his voice was strong. Firm. As if it belonged to a much younger man. Not a man well into his seventies; it was only when he spoke about Ezi that his shaky voice betrayed his age.

Mma thought of the earth falling on the coffin. Soft klomp sounds, like the heartbeat of a newborn. *Klomp. Klomp. Klomp.* The priest reciting, 'Ashes to ashes. Dust to dust.' She had to grab a handful of earth and drop it, *klomp*, on the coffin. Madam Gold grabbed a handful, *klomp*, all the while wailing hysterically. But Mma remained dry-eyed, her greatest problem being a desperate need for the toilet.

'She was buried in the cemetery,' Mma said at last. Not really answering her papannukwu's question. 'The cemetery in Enugu,' she added. There had been no need to bury her in a cemetery in another city.

'I know,' the old man said, his voice trembling. The information was enough to stop him dwelling on the death. 'My daughter buried in a cemetery! *Alu eme*. I heard that. And when I heard—' His voice broke and he kept quiet and sighed. For a long time, he did not say another word. He let out a deep groan and then said, 'We have to do another ceremony. A reburial. Give her spirit some peace.'

He must have seen the look on Mma's face for he gave her a weak smile and said, 'No, no, not what you think. We shall not be exhuming her body. Her spirit has suffered enough already. We will just have to have a reburial without her body. These things are done. My daughter cannot remain in a cemetery.' He turned his face away from Mma.

The cemetery was for people without families and for the 'lost'. When loved people died, people with families, they were buried at home. Ezi should have been resting in her ancestral matrimonial home, or lying beside her mother near the front gate of her father's house.

'Your mother was stubborn. But maybe we shouldn't have pushed her out the way we did. A man never stops loving his child. *Obala*, blood, it's a strong thing. Your grandmother and I missed her. And you. But we were not allowed to make amends. Once I had told Ezi she was no longer mine, I couldn't take it back.' He held a hand over his mouth and closed his eyes. He was silent for a while and Mma worried that he might have fallen asleep. Finally, he turned his face to Mma and spoke again. His voice rose a bit, not too much but just enough to suggest anger: 'A parent never apologises, even if he regrets his actions. It is the child who should apologise. Ezi knew that. And we waited. She knew what she had to do.'

'But what if the child doesn't regret her actions?'

'It is still her duty to apologise for getting the parent upset in the first place. Such is the nature of our world. Your mother knew it. And every day we waited and hoped. That she would go back to your father or that she would give us the chance to forgive her. But she never did either. She never gave us a chance to reconcile.'

P is for papannukwu newly excavated. Mma realised immediately that that was the precise word she had looked for when she hugged him, but had not found. His arms, frail and chafed and smelling of the earth around her neck, felt like those of some newly excavated being. He was dark, the rich darkness of a cocoa-bean, not the translucent brown of her mamannukwu in the photograph. Mamannukwu must have been light-skinned when she was younger, certainly as light-skinned as Ezi was. She wished she had met the woman. Her papannukwu's boyish frame, his demureness, the simplicity of his bedroom were at odds with Ezi's sturdiness, her loud laughter and her taste in furnishing. It was hard to believe that this man had had any hand in raising her. How odd, she thought, that she should be sitting here with someone who had watched her mother grow.

Getting here had not been easy. Madam Gold had told her that if she intended to go in search of her family, things had to be done the proper way. The Igbo way. Mma had had no idea that tradition could be so complicated.

'You do not just get up and go,' Madam Gold said. 'If you want me to, I'll set the ball rolling. All you have to do is turn up at the dates agreed. You have the addresses now. If you want me to, I will come with you.'

Yes, please: the ball could be set rolling. No, thank you: she'd rather do this on her own. But what would happen if she just turned up?

'You'd look out of place. Like one without an older person to advise her. There is no need to ruin things now with your impatience. It is only the fly without guidance that follows the corpse into the ground. *I na-egekwa m nti?* You do things properly. Do not give anyone a chance to blame your mother for not raising

109

you well. It is the dog that eats shit but it is the goat that gets rotten teeth. Are you listening to me?'

'Yes, Aunty. Thank you, Aunty.'

'Don't worry. I'm sure they'll want to see you as soon as possible. Before Christmas, you'll see them.'

First, Madam Gold had to send an envoy to Ezi's parents, hundreds of kilometres away in Aba. The envoy was made up of her husband and his friend who had both known Ezi. They said when they met Mma's papannukwu and told him why they had come, the man did not speak for a solid thirty minutes. And then he let out a loud cry of joy. *Heiiiiiijiiiiiiiiiiiiiiiiiiiiiiiiiiiiiiiii!*

Madam Gold said 'a solid thirty minutes', when she related the news to Mma. It made Mma think of this papannukwu she was yet to meet as a man of few words but with the same sense of firmness as her mother. She had not expected a man so brittle-looking. So brittle she was afraid of hugging him in case he cracked.

When she arrived, delivered by Madam Gold's driver to her grandparents' doorstep, there had been tears and plenty of singing. It was like a wedding. Aunties and uncles hugged her and passed her on until she was led inside to Papannukwu's room where the old man waited, alone and simply dressed in a cream shirt and black trousers. Once she went in, the door shut behind them to let him meet his granddaughter.

He held Mma in both hands and said several times, 'Welcome, *nwa m. Nno.*' He got up and went to the table. He opened a drawer and brought out a card with 'Wishing you the Best of the Season' written on it. He gave it to Mma and asked her to open it. A smile played on his face. Mma opened it. On each side was a sepia-coloured photograph. One was of a girl of about six or seven with knock knees and wide eyes. The other was of the same little girl holding on to a man's hand. The man wore a dark suit and carried a bowler hat under his arm. His hair was parted at the side. Both he and the girl were standing. Sitting beside them was a woman in the same print dress as the little girl. Both photographs, falling apart from age, were taped over with Sellotape. They must have been taken on the same day. Mma looked at Papannukwu and he nodded. How come she had never realised that her mother had knock knees?

'You may keep them,' he said.

'Thank you.'

'I've waited for this day for so many years. Thank you. Thank you, my daughter. The year is ending on a very good note for me. Thank you.'

The effusive gratitude embarrassed Mma. She smiled and looked down at her feet.

'You must meet your father, too, and apologise to him.'

'For?' She looked up. She could not keep the incredulity from her voice. Madam Gold had said nothing about apologising to her father.

'For your mother. It's the way of our people, my daughter. I shall send word to him. Then you must go and see him. This coming year will be one of new beginnings.'

He held her hands, turned them upwards and traced his fingers across them, as if he was reading her palms, or communicating with her in a silent language, his thumb transmitting the message he was giving her directly into her system through her skin. Then he released her.

When Papannukwu motioned for Mma to leave, and said that the others would be dying to see her, she felt like a prodigal child come home. She was led to the only vacant sofa in the sitting room, obviously reserved for her and her grandfather. The blades of the ceiling fan whirred ineffectively, losing its fight against the afternoon heat, but nobody seemed to mind. She noticed an air conditioner in the room but it did not seem to be working. The wire hanging from it was not plugged in. The plastic sheet protecting the suede cushions of the sofas from dirt squeaked with every movement. The bottles of gin Madam Gold had asked her to take along were passed around several old hands. In the middle of the room was a table with a glass top and what looked like plastic dolphins trapped inside the glass. It seemed at odds with her grandfather's style and so Mma assumed it must have been bought by one of the wives. He seemed like the sort of man to furnish his house with simple, solid, wooden furniture. Mma wondered what she ought to call her step-grandmother. She knew what she was expected to call her, but the sense of loyalty she felt for her real mamannuwku was so fierce that she resisted using the title. Besides, as nice as her step-grandmother looked (she had been one of the first to hug her and ululate that she had come), she did not feel comfortable towards her. Aunty Kelechi came forward. Her resemblance to her sister was so striking that Mma knew immediately who she was. 'You're very beautiful, Mma. Your mother raised you well. Beauty. You must meet your cousins. My daughters have always wanted a big sister. You must come and stay with us for a while.'

Mma smiled and squeezed her aunt's hands. They were soft, as if they were stuffed with cotton wool, and warm. She had received the same invitation from her uncles. All of them married with children and living in such faraway places as Langtang and Lagos. 'Come and spend Christmas with us, our sister's daughter. Let us look after you, make up for the time we did not have.'

She smiled and said, 'No thank you,' but promised to come and visit in the New Year.

'Promise?' Aunty Kelechi asked, smiling at her.

'Promise,' Mma said.

She needed time on her own. She no longer minded spending Christmas alone, now she knew there was family waiting for her.

'Ezi's spirit has sent Mma to us. We accept her apology,' Papannukwu said, addressing a photograph of his dead wife, which was being passed from hand to hand. 'Our daughter's spirit can now rest in peace. We've forgiven her!'

Mma did not miss the irony of it all. She had been so against honouring her mother's wishes, and now she was being drawn into making amends for her. Amends she was not convinced her mother had to make. But this was not the place, she realised, to voice her opinions of a parent always assuming rightness. Imagine if her mother had ever told her, 'Mma, apologise to me for everything bad I've ever done to you.' How she would have told her off. How much of a different life her mother had tried to give her. She had tried to raise her daughter with the sort of values she herself was never taught. And it hit her, like a pebble thrown on her head, why her mother could never live with her husband, not after what he did. It was not just anger at being betrayed. It was deeper than that. It was her way of challenging tradition. It was one woman taking on her world.

When the tears began to flow, they came fast, as if a tap had been turned on.

13

Christmas morning was misty and cold. Mma debated whether or not to go to church. She decided she should, to show gratitude for the turn her life had taken. Four days ago she had met her mother's family for the first time. Papannukwu had urged her to stay and spend Christmas with him but she had politely turned down the offer, saying she had not come prepared. 'I have only my handbag,' she had laughed, giddy with happiness at being wanted.

She was suffering from terrible period pains and was downing painkillers in twos and threes. She had always suffered from period pains. Backache. Cramps. Nausea. She learnt the word dysmenorrhoea before she learnt ovulation. It assaulted her every month and crippled her. But that was no reason not to go. Whenever she had her period, she was grateful she was not working and could indulge in warm showers and long lie-ins. Her mother told her once that she had suffered from it until she had Mma. Before now, that was the only thing she thought they had in common. Dysmenorrhoea.

Outside her window, she heard a mother shouting to her child to hurry up or they would be late for Mass. The mother shouted, 'You think the fada will wait for you before he starts Mass, eh?' Mma went into the bathroom and rushed a bucket bath, singing as she scrubbed her body. *La la la.* Happiness was a loud song in the bathroom. If she wanted to, she could throw her clothes in her bag and head for Aba. Or Langtang. Or Lagos. That was happiness, that knowledge.

She glanced quickly at the clock and saw that it was already quarter past seven. She was fifteen minutes late but everybody knew that the first twenty minutes was spent singing and welcoming the congregation. She had time to dress up and still make it on time for Mass. And she learnt in catechism that one was not late unless one missed the homily and, on such a day as this, the homily would take extra long. She dressed up, spread a thin layer of concealer on her face, then some foundation, and, satisfied with the velvety smoothness, dusted some powder on top. Not having anyone to make up for, she limited herself to lip gloss. By the time she got to church it was eight o'clock and the gospel reading had only just started. She slid into a bench beside a young, good-looking couple wearing matching clothes of blue lace. By this time next year, Mma thought happily, she would be at Mass with Obi, both of them dressed in matching clothes. But not lace. She would make them clothes from Ankara. Something fashionable. The couple beside her looked happy with life and Mma tried not to feel a twinge of envy. Soon, soon, she would be like them. And what was more, she would be dressed better. The blue lace did not really suit the woman. The cut of the neck was all wrong. And what was with the flared sleeves? This woman should shoot the tailor who sewed this for her, Mma thought. She realised that the gospel was over and people were sitting down. She tried to concentrate on what the priest was saying, but they were things she had heard before. The joy of Christmas. The promise of Christ's birth. An opportunity for spiritual renewal. She tried not to be bored and listened. There was no need making it to church, she thought, only to let her mind wander. The priest sounded like he was speaking from a tunnel. 'Christmas is finally here. For four weeks, we waited and we prayed for the coming blessings of Christmas. The four weeks of Advent we spent preparing for this day.'

Mma scratched behind her ear.

'Today the angels bring us news of joy for all the people, for to us is born this day in the city of David a Saviour, who is Christ the Lord, God made man. God gave up His divinity and became man for love of us. In Christ, powerful love makes itself vulnerable.' Mma was paying more attention now. She fanned herself with the bulletin she had bought at the entrance of the church. The message seemed designed for her especially. The vulnerability of love. The preparation for joy. She was glad she had come.

'This good news of great joy is for all of us. But it is very important that we make that joy our own personal joy. The question we should ask ourselves is this: How do I claim this joy for myself? How do I ensure that I flow in this joy? Let me tell you a little story, told to me by a friend of mine. A long time ago, this friend of mine, also a priest . . . Yes, we priests tend to stick together . . .'

There were trickles of laughter. He let the chuckles die out and then continued. 'This friend of mine was working in a village, *ime obodo*, one of those villages

117

forgotten by the government. They had no electricity and no pipe-borne water. The villagers walked long distances to the nearest river to quench their thirst. And then they lugged heavy buckets of water all the way back. This priest prayed and asked God to use him to ease the villagers' lives. One day he got the inspiration to sink a borehole. He called the villagers to a meeting and they discussed ways and means. He arranged a meeting with the local government chairman. Soon the borehole project had begun. Everybody was happy. Not long after, my friend was posted to a different village. One day he got a letter from his former parish with the request that he should come and visit. The borehole was working and they wanted him to see what a difference it had made to their lives. He went back to the village and rejoiced at the change. People no longer trekked for miles. They spent their time on other things. He stopped at the house of an old woman who had often cooked for him while he was a priest there. After he sat down, he begged for a cup of water, certain that this would be no trouble now the borehole was a reality. But to his surprise this old woman apologised and said, "Sorry, Fada, we have no water in the house." "Whyever not?" asked my friend. "Does the borehole not supply you?" "Indeed it does," she said, "but I am too busy to fetch water myself and my grandson refuses to go for me, preferring instead to play!"

'So you see, though the water was there for the taking, the old woman did not benefit from it. So it is with the gift of joy at Christmas. If you do not claim it, if you do not actively embrace it, if you do not seek it, you cannot benefit from it.'

Mma thought that she was already experiencing the joy. She wondered if her face glowed. She used to imagine as a child that happy people's faces shone as if they had been oiled.

'How do you benefit from it? How do you seek it? You see, Christianity is not a lazy religion. It is a religion that requires work. We still need to do something, make a little effort, before we can personally experience this joy in our lives, in our families, and in our world. It is no coincidence that the letters of "joy" are arranged the way they are. Jesus. Others, before You. That is the message of Christmas. To know joy in our lives we need to place Jesus first in everything. Secondly, we need to try to please others before trying to please ourselves. That is the recipe for joy. That is how we can convert the Christmas "Joy to the world" into a personal "Joy in my life" now and always.'

Mma's concentration was starting to wane again. She no longer had the strength to drag her mind back to the service and so she gave it free rein to go where it pleased, flitting here and there. The woman beside her shifted and Mma saw that her lace skirt was ripped at the side. She had probably not noticed. Mma laughed to herself. She would buy Ankara, Dutch wax. That seamstress on Obiagu Road performed miracles with cloth. She and Obi would even have matching shoes. They would synchronise their walk. They would look better than this couple seated beside her. And what was the woman doing putting her head on her husband's shoulder? Did she think this was their bedroom? Some people have no sense of propriety, Mma thought, wishing that a church warden would pass by and scold the couple.

As if she had read her thoughts, a purple-clad warden walked towards their aisle but she smiled at the young couple and then lashed an unsuspecting child whispering in another child's ear. The little girl's cry of pain touched Mma and she felt almost guilty for willing the warden to them. This was something that disturbed her: the liberties those church wardens took, lashing noisy kids with their koboko. How were children supposed to concentrate if Mass took so long? Even adults could not. And church wardens who spent time watching out for distracted children during service could not claim to be paying attention either. Woe betide the church warden who tried to discipline her child. Anyway, none would dare because she noticed that the wardens were selective in the children they chose to whip. They never caned ajebota children. And her children would be ajebota: children raised on butter, who wore clean ready-made clothes and went to good schools where it was a crime to speak any language but English. The church wardens stayed away from such children, pretending not to hear them talk or giggle because who knew whose children they were? Who knew what sort of power their parents had? What sort of damage they could do to a poor church warden? Instead, church wardens smiled at them. And looked for opportunities to ingratiate themselves with the parents, picking up dropped dolls and shiny plastic bags. Yes, her children would be ajebota. She had the means. They would walk into the church on Christmas morning and people would envy them.

She stared at the hastily wiped blackboards lining the church walls. St Mary's building doubled as a school. During the week children huddled into the hall, divided into classes by flat sheets of wood with legs stuck on them. For Sunday Mass, the pieces of wood were piled at the back of the hall. How could anybody learn anything in such a situation? There was no way the pieces of wood could prevent the lessons from one class filtering in to the other classrooms. She had said this once to her mother, to which the older woman responded that that was all the more reason why she, Mma, should be grateful for a mother like her who could afford to send her daughter to a proper school. St Mary's was the sort of state school where fees were low or non-existent and people sent their domestic help to assuage their guilt, knowing full well that nobody got any sort of education there. Less than one per cent of pupils who passed through St Mary's went on to get any other form of education. It simply existed as a school to salve consciences. And Mma was sure the teachers treated it as such too: wielding canes to instil discipline and doing very little else.

Remembering her mother, she thought of her father. She could hardly believe that she would be seeing him soon. In the flesh. Madam Gold has sent word that the necessary visits had been done and in eight days, she would be leaving for Kaduna. 'He's looking forward to seeing you,' she had said.

A trio of church wardens walked along the aisle, with the solemn look of executioners, their kobokos in full view. Where did one go to find people so dour-looking? So puck-faced even on Christmas Day! The homily was lasting for ever but if she went home, what was there to do? She had thought that she would have jumped at the chance to stay with her family – proper family – her aunts and uncle for Christmas but once the invitations came, she panicked. It was all too much.

'It might have done you good,' Madam Gold told her.

'They'll still be there next year,' she responded. What she did not tell her was how she had hated that they had all assumed that she had come to apologise for her mother. She imagined how her mother would have reacted to that. She could just hear her saying, 'Apologise for what? Hah! It'll be cold-cold in hell before I apologise.' She smiled and searched in her purse for money for the offertory. Congregants sang the loudest at offertory. They opened their mouths wide. They smiled and raised their voices to heaven and asked God to bless them as they gave what they could. Chickens and goats. Coins and fruit. The church, especially at Christmas, reeked of the domestic animals that had been dragged in to be offered at the altar in thanksgiving. Mma joined in the singing:

> Nwanyi mutalu nwa
> Na-enewe Anwuli
> O ku nwa ya n'aka dika Maria
> O Chukwu gozie ya, gozi kwa nwa yaaaaa.

The catechist announced that the first group of people to bring their contributions to the altar were the mothers of new babies. The mothers beamed and danced their way to the altar as if this song had been composed with them in mind, as if they were celebrating both the birth of Jesus and the birth of their babies. For the first time in her life, Mma imagined herself as a baby in her mother's arms. Had she also dragged at her mother's necklace the way a baby was now pulling at her mother's? The woman prised its fingers loose very gently and even though it would have hurt her, she nuzzled her baby's nose and carried it so that its head rested on her shoulders. Gently, she patted its buttocks and danced past.

What a long line of new mothers, Mma thought to herself. She had never noticed that her parish seemed particularly fecund. The next group was the newly married. Mma wondered if she should go. Single women were always last on the roll call. Bottom of the list, they came after couples and bachelors. Her neck was cramped and the couple beside her were affecting her mood. The woman would not sit still! The husband had gone out to the car park and come back with two chickens tied together with a red string. They were fat and they squawked heartily all the way to the altar where they joined the two bleating goats a man in a flowing agbada had dragged beside his wife and their new baby. By the time it got to the single girls Mma was hot and tired, but she persevered. She got up and danced to the altar. Anyone observing her would have seen that the glow on her face did not come from sweat. In eight days she would see her father. Her journey would come to an end.

14

The flight to Kaduna was crowded. Mma had not expected a midweek flight, on the second day of the year, to be so full. She had not thought that Kaduna was a popular destination. As the plane taxied down the runway, a passenger at the back shouted, 'Let us pray!' and without waiting for a response, immediately launched into a long prayer, ending with an 'Amen' from more than half the passengers.

She had a ball of wool in her stomach, unfurling and making her too sick to eat. An air hostess in a tight, short skirt pushed a cart beside her.

'Would you like some tea or coffee, madam?' the air hostess asked.

'Nothing, thank you.'

'Would you like a doughnut or a slice of cake?'

'Nothing. Thank you. Thanks.'

A ball of wool unravelling, reaching down from her stomach to gather at her feet and tangle around her ankles. She slipped off her shoes and pushed them under the seat in front of her. The ball became fire and spread out from her stomach to engulf every part of her. She took the in-flight magazine and began to fan herself.

It had been easy buying a ticket but it was not until she got to the airport that she found out that a ticket did not guarantee one a seat on the plane. She ignored the warning against conducting business with touts and bribed one who ensured that she got a boarding pass. Those warnings were for people who had no idea how things worked. And then she had waited for three hours before she could finally board. And all that waiting had not calmed her nerves. Instead, it had made her bite her nails like she used to as a teenager, when it annoyed her mother so much that she had often threatened to clip them off while she slept. The waiting had built up the wool in her stomach, rolling it into the huge ball it was now. She unclasped her handbag and clasped it again. It had been a mistake bringing such a huge handbag. She should have brought something smaller. She shifted in her chair and the man sitting beside her asked her if she was all right.

'Yes, I am.'

'Scared of flying?'

'No, not really.'

'God is with us. No need to be fearful,' the man said and shut his eyes.

Mma shut her own eyes but could not sleep. Bits and pieces of the conversations she had had with Madam Gold bounced around her head. 'Your mother was a very generous woman. The day we met, I'd boarded a taxi but forgotten my purse, so I could not pay the driver when he dropped me off at the market. This man, big man like that, got out of his car, held on to my wrist and swore that he'd not let me go until I'd paid him. Passers-by stopped to watch and some laughed at my humiliation. I begged this man to take me home so I could retrieve my purse. He refused. See me, all dressed up, crying and begging. I had no idea what else to do when a total stranger, a woman not much younger than me, walked up to the driver, asked him how much I owed and paid him off. She insisted on lending me the money for my shopping that day.'

'E always wanted the best for you. She loved you without reservation.'

'Your father still lives in Kaduna. In the same house. Finding him was as easy as buying salt.'

Mma opened her eyes. She looked out of the window and saw Kaduna spread out below her.

The landing was the smoothest Mma had ever experienced. It was a landing on silk. The passengers erupted into spontaneous applause and Mma joined them. The man beside her woke up with a start and then smiled sheepishly. 'Ah, thank God for His journey mercies. I can never stay awake on a plane. You live in Kaduna?' he asked.

'No, my father does. I'm visiting him.'

F is for father. To say F properly, the lower lip has to come between the upper teeth and the lower teeth. Not imprisoned, but lightly trapped and then instantly released as if it were being teased by a lover. F was her father. Should she call him Father? Or Papa? Or Daddy? Or Dad? Madam Gold had said the right word would come to her, there was no need to get herself worked up worrying which was best. When she had asked Obi over the phone, he'd told her that she was just being silly, worrying over such a little thing.

'Are there big things I should worry about, then?' she had asked. Should she worry about whether he would accept her? Love her? Want her?

'A parent's love is a given,' Obi had said. 'No need to worry about that either.'

F is for father. A father who loved you just because. Even if you had been absent from his life since you were a baby.

Kaduna was more modern than she had expected. It was like Enugu on a bigger scale. She imagined the welcome. She remembered the off-hand way she had tried to say 'father' to the man on the plane, easy, so that the man noticed nothing of her anxiety. F is for father.

The taxi driver asked if she was new to the city. She said she was. He kept a running commentary of the city sights as he drove but she hardly paid him any attention. She had never been a good tourist and today was not the right day to start. She kept her eyes glued to the window, her hands busy working the clasp of her bag. The house he deposited her in front of was old and imposing. Even in its run-down state, it was still easy to see the shadow of its former magnificence. The gate was unmanned and so when the taxi dropped her off, she had pushed it open herself and walked to the front door. She had refused Aunty Kelechi's offer to accompany her. This was something she had to do herself, she said. But now that she was here, she suddenly wished there was somebody there to hold her hand. She felt like a child on her first day at school. There had been an offer made to meet her at the airport but she had declined that, too. Maybe, she thought now, she should have accepted it.

She had told herself that she did not want any fuss made, not the way that her visit to Aba had been turned into a carnival. Yet she was somewhat disappointed that the compound seemed indifferent to her arrival. There were no nervous family members pacing beyond the gate waiting to catch a first glimpse of her; there were no balloons festooned to the balcony to show that this was an important occasion. She walked slowly to the door, dragging the small suitcase she had packed with presents she had bought (guided again by Madam Gold) and the few outfits she would need for her visit.

Last night, she had the dream of her mother again. This time, she looked less filleted, as if she had been stuffed up where the flesh was previously scooped out. But the whiff of otapiapia remained, clinging to her fiercely like a devoted dog; Mma could still smell it when she woke. It made her weep for things she was not yet ready to face. The weight of it was too much, too huge to confront. The hand she raised to ring the doorbell was heavy and shaky, as if she carried dumb-bells way beyond her strength. She brought a thumb to the button and pressed harder than she had meant to. She could hear the bell ringing. It was loud and angry. It jarred. The door swung in to reveal a thick-waisted woman in a too-long skirt and a too-white lace blouse with silver sequins. This was Rapu. The other woman in her father's life.

Part 2

Azu na-enoro ibe ya adiro ebu ibu.

A fish that does not swallow other fishes does not grow fat.

Igbo proverb

Lokpanta, 1960s

1

When Rapu was born, Mmeri, the expert midwife and certified soothsayer from down the road, took the umbilical cord between her stubby fingers, rolled it beside her ear, sunk her teeth into it, spat on it and gave it to the baby's father to bury with the words, 'She shall lead you away from hunger. Ugani has left your household. Famine shall never visit you again. It is gone.'

She wiped the smear of blood from her lips with the back of her palm and proclaimed, 'This is the one you've all been waiting for. She has come. Your wait is over. The time has come to rejoice.'

Echewa dug a hole beside the orange tree in the middle of the compound and buried the umbilical cord there, then he ran back into his wife's room, his face one broad grin. In a fit of ecstasy, he insisted – much to the chagrin of his visiting mother-in-law – on cooking the yam porridge his wife must eat to warm her stomach.

'What nonsense is this?' she grumbled as she watched him slice the yam and soak the white slices in water, flinging the too-thick pieces into the pot so that it splattered water on the firewood. She ran behind him and gathered the skin he had peeled onto the kitchen floor. She almost slipped on one. 'How can I be here and you do the cooking for Mgboji? How does it reflect on me?' He ignored her, and reached for the palm oil.

'What man cooks for his wife? This is a woman's job. That's why I've come!' His strong arms, unused to the femininity of kitchen work, spilled oil on the floor and knocked down the basket of fish hanging from the rafter, and got his mother-in-law grumbling even louder as she mopped and picked up after him. He would not be stopped. She pricked her finger on a fishbone and said, '*Biko nu*, stop', her voice never rising to match her anger, maintaining a respectful diffidence of tone. He might be her son-in-law, but he was head of the household. He ignored her. He reached out for a wrap of okpei and knocked the metal cup off the clay pot. His mother-in-law, careful not to let herself be heard, muttered something about men who interfered in the woman's world. Echewa laughed as if the cup had told him a private joke, kicked it in amusement and shouted, 'Yes!', like a football player who had just scored the winning goal.

He already had two children. It had taken the birth of the third for Mmeri to see a change in their future.

With tears in her eyes and still shivering with the cold that comes from a delivery, Rapu's mother shouted out for her mother from the bedroom. Her new baby lay on her stomach. She asked her mother to ensure that the soothsayer was sent home with the only chicken in the house. It was a chicken they had been saving for the baby's naming ceremony, but who better to give it to than Mmeri who had brought them words of hope? Mmeri whose confirmation that their days of poverty were over.

★　　★　　★

134

Mmeri, corpulent and smiling, accepted the chicken and swung it, dangling on one leg, all the way home, where it went into a huge pot of egusi soup, spiced with the reddest of peppers and served with a bowl of pounded yam, big enough to feed two grown men. Helping to birth a child was a demanding task. It always made her hungry. At hand was a large calabash of fresh palm wine which she washed down the food with. Mmeri drank like a man: taking huge gulps, hardly ever stopping to draw breath. By the time her wine was finished, her prophecy had already gone round the village. In Lokpanta good news spread just as fast as bad. People were as eager to celebrate as they were to commiserate. News provided them with free drinks and a chance to contemplate the world.

People said what a blessing it was. They had suffered enough. The baby had come into a family notorious for their bad luck and it was only right that their fortunes should change. Visitors streamed in and out to take a look at the miracle child. They said how beautiful she was. Those old enough to remember said how very much like her great-grandmother she looked. The eyes – a bit slanted – were definitely the old woman's. Maybe she had come back. Tired of watching her grandson suffer to feed his family, she had nagged the gods until they decided the time was ripe for her reincarnation. The villagers held her little hands, looked into her eyes and said how wise they looked, no doubt about it. The newborn was definitely Echewa's grandmother. They named her Big Mother and whispered messages for her to take to their ancestors (it was common knowledge that babies, newly born, still had a connection with the world they had just left). And the visitors were fed with what little Echewa had. And palm wine flowed and visitors drank and loosened their tongues and prayed for more blessings on the family who gave generously. And Echewa said how much more they would give once the riches that were due them eventually materialised.

Some said they had always known a day like this would come, the change in Echewa's fortune snaking into their dreams while they slept at night. People laughed out loud and hit Echewa's back in joviality and pinched the baby's cheeks. But Echewa and his wife, wise in the ways of their people, knew that not everybody who laughed with you rejoiced with you. They knew that even at times like these, there were those with evil hands and evil eyes who tried to steal your fortune and transfer it to themselves or throw it into the River Mmavu so that your good luck was gone for ever and ever. So Echewa and his wife carried ugolo in their cheeks to ward off evil and hid a sachet of the bitter kola under the baby's pillow. Its efficacy in keeping evil at bay was not to be doubted. Last tapping season, Echewa had fallen off a palm wine tree. Somehow, the rope around him, holding him to the tree, had unknotted (who had ever heard of such a thing?). It was obvious it was the handiwork of an evil person who wanted him dead (although why anyone would want to kill a poor man like him was completely beyond him) and he had fallen to what should have been his death, or at best a broken leg. Luckily, that day, not only was his god awake, but Echewa had ugolo in his mouth, and had ended up with nothing worse than a stubbed toe. A stubbed toe! He shouted whenever he told the story, such was his surprise.

Seven days after the birth the baby was presented to the village and named with a drop of local gin on her forehead. The villagers said it was a sensible name, Rapu. It was a name that asked the ill luck to go away and never return. Rapu. Go away. A name that banished the ill luck to a hole deep enough to swallow it and keep it down. For as everyone knew, names had as much influence on one's future as the gods did. It was like meeting the gods halfway, which was why an entire week was needed to think of a name both apt and beautiful. And for a family like theirs, Rapu was really the most appropriate name. They could not have chosen a better one. The gods – even the Christian God the family had newly discovered – were bound to be happy with the choice.

2

The story was repeated to Rapu several times during her childhood. Of how she had found favour with the gods, of how she would take the family out of its penury. Nobody doubted the midwife's words, or the veracity of Ajofia's prophecy, which he had delivered with the confidence of one in direct contact with the gods. Ajofia had assured Echewa that Rapu would make a fortune for the family. What was not clear was how Rapu was to go about seeing to its fulfilment. It was generally believed that she would stumble upon it, for the ways of the gods are mysterious, but it was also generally known that the gods expect a certain amount of initiative. It was the least a human being could do. The gods do not just say, '*Ngwa*, let me. Open your mouth. Open wide, let me feed you,' even though they have the power to do so. No. If you want to eat the food that has been destined for you, you have to open your mouth yourself. 'Open wide and you'll be fed,' Echewa reminded his family.

More importantly, the gods' favourite had to be kept happy, for if she was happy, then the gods were happy too. You did not treat a king's heir with derision and expect rewards. Not even the compassionate Christian God would accept it. The pastor had told them the story of a landowner who had a plantation full of palm trees. Then he leased it to tenants and went to live in another village. When palm-wine season came, the landowner sent his slaves to the tenants to collect his produce. But the tenants seized his slaves; they beat one, killed another, and stoned another. Again he sent other slaves, more than the first time; and they were treated in the same way. Finally he sent his son to them, saying, 'They will respect my son.' But when the tenants saw the son, they said to themselves, 'This is the heir; come, let us kill him and get his inheritance.' So they seized him, threw him out of the vineyard, and killed him. 'Now when the owner of the plantation comes, what will he do to those tenants?' the pastor asked. The congregation shouted as one, 'He'll kill them all!' Echewa knew this and so he saw to it that the gods were kept happy.

Whenever the family ate yam, Rapu got the middle part, the part reserved for honoured guests. When the family ate fish, Rapu got its head. She enjoyed prising out the little eyes, pellets of white, and chewing on them until her jaws ached. It was much more fun than chewing the gum from an udala fruit.

'When I become rich, I shall eat fish every day!' she told her mother. And the response was always, 'When you become rich, we shall all eat chicken and goat meat. No more fish.'

Fish was for the poor, for those who were one step away from having entirely nothing. The rich men, all the ones with thick necks and huge bellies, gorged on chicken every Sunday, and on beef and goat every other day of the week. Their children did not fight over a chicken head because there were enough chicken heads to go around. The meat eaters had skin that shone like magic and everybody who was wise yearned to be like them. Rapu did not dare tell her mother that she did not want to give up fish.

School was a torture for Rapu. Teachers complained that she talked too much, laughed too loud and snatched other pupils' property: pencils, rubbers, chalk for their slates. Hardly a day went by when she was not at the top of the noisemakers' list. Her buttocks hurt from the thrashings from her class teacher who flogged like a cattle herder.

Yet she was unrepentant. And not bright. Primary Science confused her (if man descended from monkeys, how come the monkey that lived with Mama Boy near the church, and has lived with her for as long as anyone remembered, has not evolved and become human?) and grammar baffled her even more (she could never grasp why it was 'Run Run Ran' but 'See Saw Seen'). When she was caned by her teacher for failing to conjugate the verb Fear (she had said 'Fear Fore Forn'), she decided that school was not for her. There was no logic in what she read, all the teaching seemed designed both to compound her problems and to confound her. When she asked questions, her teachers told her off for being disruptive. How could it be 'Tear Tore Torn'? Change the first letter and the rules changed completely! How was she supposed to remember all of that? 'See Saw Sawn'. It was an unrealistic demand. And on top of that there was the illogicality of mathematics to deal with. Finding solutions to abstract questions that had nothing to do with real life. She did not see how any of this would help her, how it would help anybody really.

After her second year at the local mission school, she broke her chalk-stained slate and told her parents she never wanted to go back. Her father saw this as a sign of resilient independence, an indicator that she had the strength of will required to pursue all their dreams, and was glad, frankly, not to have to spend money on school fees for her. She did not need an education to save them. Her mother rested her eyes on her fading wrapper and dreamt of a day when she could afford a brand-new one; something in vogue, fashionable, like some of the women she knew. If the girl did not want to go to school, let her stay at home, her father declared magnanimously, beaming with pride. Let her stay here and learn what she needs to learn. The boys can stay on. They don't seem to want to learn anything outside of school anyway. His sons infuriated him with their timidity, their keenness to swallow the rubbish they were taught. Neither boy had a questioning mind, an itch to get out in the world and make money.

The daughter should have been his son and the sons should have been daughters but life did not ask you what you wanted, did it? It showed you its arse and plopped its shit where it wanted. Nothing anyone could do about that. You took the shit and you did what you could do with it. His sons had no backbone so school was maybe the best place for them. They had soft palms and weak feet: they would only fare well in government offices where they could wear shoes and socks all day, and so let them continue with school and maybe it would make them important men too.

And so her brothers, Eze and Aru, toiled on, mastering the square roots of numbers and learning what the difference was between a prime number and an ordinary number, while they waited patiently for Rapu to rescue them from the poverty in which they were mired (and went to school in threadbare uniforms that were handed down to them by well-meaning neighbours). When they complained of hunger, their father reminded them that the hunger that has hope of being assuaged does not kill. Patience was all that was needed, for their luck to turn. Patience, and a visit to Ajofia, two villages away, to ensure that no evil eye came between his family and what belonged to them.

Ajofia, dying and shaky, was still well respected for the efficacy of his juju. Even those who converted to Christianity still made the nightly trips to Ajofia to listen to him consult their forefathers on their behalf. There were certain things, they said, beyond the grasp of a Western God. And if you were *onyesiemens* like Echewa, you knew that the Anglican God was a lot more amenable, a lot more flexible than the Catholic God (who demanded celibacy from His priests), and would not mind if you went to Ajofia. Echewa was told what to buy, what to sacrifice, and to keep secret what had been told to him until such a time when it no longer needed to be a secret.

Rapu grew: spindly legged and flat-chested even when her friends were starting to sprout breasts. Ajofia was by now long dead and Echewa was starting to despair when a townsman and his wife drove into their compound one day in the middle of the rainy season, with a request that assured the despairing man that all would, after all, be well. He reminded his wife, 'When God creates an itch He creates the fingernails with which to scratch it.'

142

Their fingernails for the itch that had worried them for years had finally arrived.

Echewa offered them two stools to sit on under the shade of an orange tree and they thanked him and sat. 'I am Mike,' the man said, folding up the sleeves of his shirt. 'This is my wife, Ezi. We hope you can help us.'

'As long as it doesn't involve killing a human being, I'll see what I can do.'

'No, oo. No killing involved,' Mike said. 'We hope it is something that will be of mutual benefit to us.' When he stated their mission and saw in the way Echewa hid a smile that they would be successful, they were happy. Mike saw Ezi's shoulders relax. She wanted this, and he wanted it for her.

'My wife is not home,' Echewa said, shouting for Rapu. 'Do you know when your mother will return?'

'No, sir.'

'Won't you greet our visitors?'

Rapu curtsied and said, 'Nno. Gu aftunun.' She looked at the visitors' clothes, their covered shoes, comparing them to her father's bare feet.

'Rapu is a wonderful daughter,' Echewa said. 'She must have been a man in a previous life. Her frame hides an incredible strength. She is a match for any boy her age. The year she left school, she beat up a boy who threatened all the girls. Rapu is strong, oo, *o sili ike*. She has only one bone! *Ofu okpukpu!*' He dismissed his daughter and turned to the guests.

'Did she finish school?' Mike asked.

'No. No need for school. What does a girl need school for? My sons are eating all the education this family needs. They dream of big jobs in the city. I've told them they can go: you do not stand in one place to watch a masquerade. They can go, but not far. Maybe Enugu. Or even Onitsha. It is a problem these days – all our young men who ought to keep their fathers' homesteads are leaving for the cities and forgetting their roots. But you don't seem to be one of them. You go home often, do you?'

'Yes,' Mike said, scratching his neck to get rid of an ant that was traipsing along his collar.

'So many homesteads abandoned. And you can't even blame the Church. Many people here are Anglican. The pastor lets us respect the spirit of our fathers. His God is closer to the one our fathers worshipped. The Catholic God is stiff. Too stiff! Only understands His people when they pray in a foreign language! He leaves no room to manoeuvre at all. You know what the Catholic fada tells them every Sunday? That his God is a jealous God. He does not like to share with others. Now, isn't the heaven wide enough for as many gods as want to fit in?' He laughed and the visitors smiled politely. 'Isidu died last year and his son refused to pour libation to their family god. Nobody does such a thing and expects good. His father's spirit is haunting him now! He's gone mad in the big city. I hear he's lost his job, lost his wife, lost everything! You know what they say: the fly that refuses to heed the advice of his elders follows the corpse into the ground. But you two look like sensible people. Very sensible. How was the city when you left it?'

'Good,' Mike answered.

'The city is a tempter,' Echewa said, shaking his head. 'The city is like a beautiful woman that lures men to their destruction. It's like *mamywata*. It's taken our men away and turned them into fools. But you two don't look like fools. You look very sensible. Ah, here I am talking and forgetting to offer you anything. Please forgive me. What can I offer you? A cup of water? I have no palm wine in the house but if you come back tomorrow I will have the best to be found in Lokpanta waiting for you. Sweet, sweet like sugar when fresh but potent like gin by evening. There is no one whose palm wine comes close to that of Papa Bomboy's. But tomorrow, you'll be able to try it for yourselves and tell me whether I've spoken the truth or not.'

'That would be great,' Mike said. He was looking forward to buying some palm wine to take back with him to Kaduna, he added.

A dog strayed into the compound, looked at the three people sitting under the tree, and walked towards them. Echewa bent from his stool, picked up a stick and flung it at the dog. '*Cha!* Go away, you shit-eater!'

'My wife likes dogs,' Mike said, and looked almost apologetically at Ezi. The dog ran a short distance and then came back, tail between its legs.

Echewa laughed. 'In our village you chase dogs away unless there is faeces for them to eat. It should go to homes where they have young children who defecate on the floor. Mine are grown. I've done my bit. We are not like you city people who I hear even sleep with dogs in the same room. That's what the city does. It makes people unable to draw the line between man and beast. Sleeping with a dog in your room, *tufia!* Abomination.' He spat and it landed on the dog's paw. It licked it.

Ezi looked at her husband. 'It's time for us to go. We will come back tomorrow,' said Mike.

'Yes, yes. Tomorrow is a good day. The girl's mother will be here then. This is not a decision I can take alone.' He rubbed his palms together as he spoke, as if the action meant something infinitely more than what he was saying.

'Come back tomorrow and try the best palm wine our village has to offer. If anybody tells you their palm wine is better than Papa Bomboy's, tell them I said they are incorrigible liars. Yes! Tell them I said so.' He rubbed his hands again as the couple stood up. 'Yes, come back tomorrow and talk to the girl's mother too. She must be present.'

Echewa walked them out and watched as the car in all its revving glory drove away, leaving tracks on the sand, criss-crossing with the marks left by the brooms that Rapu and her mother had used to sweep only hours earlier. Somehow the combination of the thin long strokes left by the broom and the strong marks left by the car created a pattern more life-affirming, more solid than any Echewa had ever seen. He shouted for Rapu as he made his way back to his spot under the tree, whistling a tune that made him smile. And Rapu saw the world slide off his shoulders in one huge earth-shattering chunk. And she saw the glitter, the shine in his eyes, and knew that he was unutterably proud of her. And so she smiled too and this man who was not easily given to physical shows of affection held out his hands for her to walk into, and hugged her.

3

The couple came back the next day as they said they would. This time they came with bottles of schnapps and a bundle of money to show their good will. And to show how thoughtful they were, they also brought loaves of bread and two tins of margarine for the family. 'You didn't have to!' Echewa said, but he and his family were touched by their generosity.

The man spoke in private with Echewa. When they finished talking, Echewa called Rapu. She was washed and oiled, her face shining from Vaseline and her hair combed and groomed. She was a woman on a mission, her father joked, telling how she had hardly slept all night, how she had insisted on wearing her Christmas dress. After all, going to the city was as good an occasion as any to wear one's best dress: a cotton affair with a bodice of lace which was too big everywhere. She swam in the dress.

In the presence of the visitors, Echewa gave her titbits of wisdom. 'Behave yourself in the city and you'll bring honour not only on our family but on yourself as well. Walk like a chameleon in the city. Adapt to their ways but remember who you are.' Her mother had given her own words of advice the way women do: discreetly, whispering into her daughter's ears, as if she were afraid that if she spoke them out loud, some evil person or thing would spirit them away before they reached Rapu's ears. Rapu had to be focused, do her job conscientiously. 'Do not get tempted by the evils of the city, by all its lights. Remember the family you've left behind. Be like the tortoise: clever and careful.'

Rapu's father had prepared well for his visitors this time. He had palm wine and food. He served the palm wine from a wooden calabash. 'Papa Bomboy's *mmanya nkwu!* Drink it and tell me whether you've had palm wine that tasted as good as this! Tell me whether I spoke the truth about it or not!'

The man flicked off an ant with his little finger, took a gulp and smiled. 'This is indeed very good wine. Very good!'

'I told you so!'

Echewa handed the woman a cup. She was more hesitant, taking only a tentative sip. She said nothing.

Then Rapu and her mother came in bearing trays of food and water. There was gari and egusi soup. The couple washed their hands in the bowl of water Rapu held out to them and began to eat. 'Very delicious soup!' the man said. His wife nodded her approval.

Echewa said, 'Rapu's the best cook in Lokpanta. Anyone who tells you otherwise is a liar! Tell them I, Echewa, said so. You're lucky to be getting her. The girl's cooking can make anyone overeat! I used to think no one could surpass my wife's cooking but her daughter has outdone her. Eat the food and tell me whether you've had any tastier than Rapu's.'

'It is excellent,' the man said, licking his fingers. His wife said nothing, concentrating on moulding delicate balls of gari to dip in the bowl of soup.

'Your *nwanyi* eats like a bird!' Echewa said, laughing. 'City women! They do not have the appetite of their village colleagues. My wife would have finished that plate of food by now!' He laughed loud.

When the visitors finished eating and the plates were cleared and the promise had been given that Rapu would be sent back twice a year on holiday to visit her parents, it was time to go. Rapu went into an inner room and came out with a plastic bag of clothes. Her mother did not walk with them to the car but stood back at the door, a hand covering her mouth, as if she were trying to stop herself from shouting. Rapu's brothers walked her to the car. When they arrived her father exclaimed that he had almost forgotten the presents he had. 'Eze and Aru, run back and bring the gifts from the kitchen. How terrible it would have been had I forgotten! *Ngwa*, hurry up, the journey is far and they need to set out soon.' He half pushed Eze, who scrambled off after his brother and presently came back dragging bags of fruit and vegetables: oranges, guava, dark-skinned pears covered in sand, ears of fresh corn, some oranges. Tubers of yam and a bag of cocoyams.

The man said it was all too much. 'Too much. Thank you. You're very kind.' He opened the boot and helped the boys load the presents into it, then opened the back door and gestured to Rapu to climb in and sit down, they had to get going or they would have to sleep in Enugu and he did not want that.

Her father looked satisfied with the magnanimity of his gifts. Rapu's mother had complained the day before when he got the presents ready that he was giving away too much – after all, their daughter was going with them, too – but now as Echewa felt the bulk of the money he had just received in his shirt pocket he did not regret his generosity. It matched theirs. He smiled again.

The couple told her to call them Uncle and Aunty. The man drove and the woman sat beside him. Rapu sat alone in the back, her palms face down on the seat under her buttocks, trying not to bounce from excitement at the thought of a new adventure.

She watched the village disappear through the wound-down windows of the car. This was not the first time she had been in a car, but it was the first time she could see beyond the ears of the passengers she was sandwiched between. Before now, her trips (in the public bus when she accompanied her mother to Awgu market) involved being squashed between her mother and another passenger who might or might not be carrying baskets of food or chickens to sell, or which they had just bought, rubbing skins with the passengers, their sweat mixing with hers. Once the chicken that a woman beside her was holding escaped and shat on her. She always got off the bus itching for a bath. Now, she could stretch out if she wanted to, she could look out as her old life disappeared in a puff of dust and the car sailed its way from the village onto the highway.

It began to rain soon after and Uncle Mike put the windows up. The windscreen wipers swished to and fro, to and fro, sweeping sheets of rain away and Rapu followed the toing and froing, the toing and froing with her eyes, transforming the swishing sound into a rhythm in her head. The rain did not let up as they got to

Enugu, a good hour's drive away, where they were making a stop to see a relative of Uncle Mike's: a round man whom Aunty Ezi did not seem overly fond of. She grumbled about 'interfering family' as they stopped in front of his house. Uncle Mike told her that he meant well, and, after all, he, Mike, was not one to let his family come between himself and his wife. Had she forgotten how he had handled the problem with his mother? And with Egbuna? And Rapu was shocked to hear the woman retort that she hoped it stayed that way because Silas was a vile man. 'Your mother and your brother are different. Silas is worse. He is a snake. *Agwo!*'

In Lokpanta women did not speak to their husbands like that. If they disagreed they saved their anger and their words for when they were with their fellow women. How often had Rapu heard her mother and her friends challenging their husbands in the safety of their kitchens, saying how much they disagreed with a certain viewpoint or opinion? Yet they would go ahead with their men's wishes: visit that in-law they did not like at all; look after that mother-in-law who was certainly a witch; accept that son their husband had with another woman. No one she knew would complain so brazenly about their husband's family. Ah, she thought to herself, her education into the city's ways had already begun; her bag of tales was already filling up. It was Rapu's first glimpse of a big city and she was not impressed. All those hills looked like the monstrous breasts of a giantess. And the sky seemed sullied, as if people had eaten and had wiped their hands on the clouds. Silas's house did nothing to redeem the city: it was in dire need of a lick of paint. Where Rapu had expected cleanliness and order, she found chaos and dirt. In front of Silas's house was a gutter that stank like something had lain dead in it since the beginning of creation. They crossed the gutter and walked into a courtyard peopled with children playing with a tattered ball. The courtyard led into a dark, grimy passage with a series of doors. It smelt suspiciously of a goat farm. If this was the city, it was a major let-down. She could not understand how people could live like this, with such dirt. She had thought the city was dustless, spotless, full of space, with people all dressed up walking around the whole day. Why all the fuss if this was all there was to it? Why did people in the village talk of it as if it were next door to heaven? Why did her friends constantly dream of leaving? And all the stories of the city she had heard, where had they sprung from? If there was another side to the city, a better side, then there was still some hope that the couple she was with would live there. Or maybe Kaduna was not like Enugu. Maybe that was more of a city. Maybe Kaduna would live up to the expectations which had made her dress in her Sunday best so that she did not look out of place.

Silas lived in a ground-floor flat, his sitting-room walls covered with pictures of children with old faces. Rapu counted. Six. Silas and Uncle Mike shook hands and exchanged greetings. He turned to Aunty Ezi. 'Our wife, are you inviting us soon?' Aunty Ezi ignored him, although for a minute it looked like she was going to answer, going to say something caustic in return. It was on her face.

The six children were called in to greet the visitors. They arrived dripping water on the floor. Uncle Mike patted the heads of the girl and her five brothers and said they should take care not to play for too long in the rain, and then fumbled in his pocket for some 'change for popcorn'. Aunty Ezi responded to their greeting but said nothing else and they, by the by, filed out with whoops of joy at the money they had received. Rapu could imagine them showing off to their playmates in the courtyard.

Silas asked what they would like to drink, but Uncle Mike said they were on their way to Kaduna and had better be off, they only stopped by to show him their faces. And where was his wife? They had hoped to see her.

'Jekene has gone to spend time with her sister in Akpugo. You know her youngest sister, Mmutaka?'

Without waiting for a response, he continued. 'Mmutaka has just had her eighth baby. Very fertile women in that family,' he said, as if he was passing on some important information. Neither Uncle Mike nor Aunty Ezi said anything in response.

'It is very good that you remember the customs of our place,' Silas said. He looked at Aunty Ezi with a face like he unexpectedly sucked on a lemon. 'At least take a kola nut. Take it home if you can't eat it now. You can't show me your faces and then go away with nothing, as if you've come to an empty house. I may not be rich but I can still be hospitable.' He went into an inner room and came out with five kola nuts on a saucer. Uncle Mike thanked him and gave him back the saucer. Silas took a kola nut, prayed over it and broke it into four lobes. He took a lobe and asked Uncle Mike and Aunty Ezi to take one each. And then he made Uncle Mike take the remaining kola nuts and store them in his pocket. As they got up to leave, Uncle Mike pulled out a wad of notes and dropped it in the saucer in which the kola nuts had come. 'For the children,' he said and Silas gave him a wide smile. 'May the pocket from which the money has come never run dry.'

As soon as they got into the car, Aunty Ezi turned to her husband. 'Despicable man. He can't look after the multitude he has and he has the guts to worry about someone else's childlessness? Am I God, Mike? Am I God?' Her voice was rising now so that it filled the car and bounced all over the empty spaces. She asked again, '*A bum Chukwu?* Am I God?'

'Don't let him bother you,' her husband said.

'Easy for you to say,' she answered. 'Easy for you to say.'

4

Rapu hoped the rain would not follow them to Kaduna. It would not be a very auspicious start to her brand-new life. She worried now, especially after her glimpse of Enugu, that Kaduna would be a monumental disappointment. Even the coolness of the car had lost its novelty, having been somewhat dampened by the gutters of Enugu. How disappointed her father would be. She sat in the back next to the plastic bag containing her clothes and a bale of wrapper that her mother had inexplicably given her just before they departed. Like all of her mother's wrappers, this was not new. It was faded from several washings and from age. Rapu had no idea what she was supposed to do with it. The reason would come, she was sure. After all, it was said that her mother's family had the gift of the second eye. They saw things ordinary people were not privy to.

The story was still being told of how her mother's grandmother (before she converted and became Christian) used stones to tell the future. She was a powerful rain-maker too, and could also sweep away the clouds with a short broom on special occasions when the villagers needed it to remain dry. When people got married, they came and begged her to keep the rain at bay until after their ceremonies. Her fame even spread beyond Lokpanta to other villages: Lokpaukwu, Okigwe, Mgbo, Uturu. The pastor had convinced her to convert to Christianity with gifts and an assurance that she would make it to his God's heaven, but what had clinched the deal was the position of church warden. She liked the purple sashes they wore and the authority they wielded. As part of the deal, she cast her rain stones into the River Mmavu and scattered the broom onto her cooking fire. People said the fire cackled and gave out a sound like the mournful cries of an old woman. The food cooking on top of it burned.

Aunty Ezi, whose delicate smell filled Rapu's nose, sat in the passenger seat while her husband drove. She had not said much when they came to see Rapu's father and had only given a cursory nod to Rapu's greeting. It was Uncle Mike who had done all the talking. Aunty Ezi's only comment had been on Rapu's size. 'She's small. I'm not sure she'll do.'

Her father had assured her. 'She's not as young as she looks. Look at her ankles. That's the way to know a woman's real age. She takes after her mother. All small and fragile-looking, but believe me, they can take on any male their age in a fight and win.'

Aunty Ezi had looked like she would burst out in laughter but Uncle Mike had asked, 'How old is she?'

'If I am not mistaken, she will be thirteen before the rainy season ends. It is a pity her mother is not here to confirm it but, you see, she had to go to a meeting in the church.'

Uncle Mike had said they believed him and everybody had laughed. His voice was strong and Rapu liked that.

Rapu watched him now and worried at the lazy way he held the steering wheel. Nwogu, whose truck sometimes ferried the villagers to the market, always held the steering wheel with the seriousness it deserved. Uncle Mike's casualness worried Rapu almost as much as the rain. He sat back into his chair and held the wheel with one careless hand.

The bothersome rain did not let up as they entered Makurdi, sounding like pebbles on the roof of the car, splashing hard against the windscreen. Rapu tried to forget her worry by losing herself again in the swish-swashing of the wipers as they beat to keep up with the increasing downpour.

Makurdi looked like a city in prayer. There was a stillness to it that she had not expected to find in a city. But she preferred it to what she had seen of Enugu. She looked out of her window. The few people she saw scurrying away from the rain hidden under huge umbrellas seemed vague, the way ghosts were said to be. Her friend Kasiam saw a ghost once. She said it was not skeletal like in the stories her mother told, but fleshed out like a human being and blurred, so Kasiam could not make out whose ghost it was. It might have been her long-departed father.

'Why didn't you slice his cheek with a razorblade to keep him with you?' Rapu had asked. If you cut a ghost's cheek it would no longer be able to return under the earth but would forever stay with you. Kasiam had said that, not being sure it was her father, she had not dared. 'What if it was the ghost of a stranger? Of a wicked stranger?' And she had a point. Nobody wanted the

157

responsibility of a stranger's ghost. Plus, if it was a wicked stranger you took on all the punishment for its wickedness on earth. Thinking of the dead made her scared. It wasn't ghosts of people you knew that scared you, but ghosts of people who had been strangers, who had owed you nothing in life. Her grandparents had died before she was old enough to know them. And now she had left home she was suddenly seized with the fear that someone close to her would die before she had a chance to see them again. This fear displaced her excitement and she reached instinctively for her mother's wrapper and held it to her nose, inhaling the sharp, smoky, old-wrapper smell of her mother. The wrapper had been given to her so that she could carry familiar smells with her, to console her.

Rapu was asleep when they entered Kaduna. By the time she woke, the rain had stopped and their car had slowed down, joining a traffic jam that stretched languorously along well-tarred roads. Kaduna looked cleansed. Like a Catholic who had just come away from a confession. This pleased her. The cleanliness she could spy. Inside the car no one talked. The radio played a soft tune which splintered into silence as they pulled up in front of a massive gate.

She wondered who they had come to pay obeisance to. The house behind the gate peeped out, and did not look like a house in which people lived. Maybe it was a cathedral of some sort. A honk of the horn and the gates were swung open by a middle-aged man in a skull cap. His shouted 'Welcome' was muted by the wound-up windows. He ran behind and as soon as they stopped, opened the boot to empty it of the fruit and vegetables they had brought along with them. He heaved out bags and put them on the floor beside the car.

The house was magical. Bigger than any of the other houses surrounding it, bigger than the Catholic cathedral in Lokpanta built with funding from the Europeans. This house was big enough to accommodate an entire village and was nothing like Rapu had ever dreamt of. She did not even think the world had enough money to erect such buildings. Surely this could not be her new home. But she was going to be living here. And for a moment excitement surged through her. It was perhaps the excitement of the thought that gave her a pressing need to urinate, and she whispered conspiratorially to Aunty Ezi who was now out of the car and pressing against her husband in a rather brazen embrace.

Having always lived in a village where pit latrines were all there was, definitely one step above doing your business in the bush with thorns scratching your bare buttocks, the toilet was a fairytale. It looked good enough to eat in. She gazed at the pristine whiteness of it all and wondered where to start. Should she stand on it? Stoop over it? Sit? Where does one begin with such things? She wondered, she touched, and she looked at Aunty Ezi who with a laugh showed her what to do. What to open. How to sit. 'And please flush it when you are done. Just twist this handle here and the job is done. Then you come out and help Silvanus bring in the things.'

They took her on a tour around their house after the car had been emptied. The house was carpeted from head to toe. There was no question about it: these people were rich. Even by city standards.

'If you show me where the utensils are, Aunty, I can start cooking,' Rapu offered as the tour ended. She knew how to behave like a proper maid and was determined that they knew it too. She did not want them changing their minds about her, like the city people who had taken her friend Kasiam last year did. Kasiam did not last one day. When they brought her back to her widowed mother who lived two compounds away from Rapu's family, the shamed woman lamented loudly of all she had effectively lost: the monthly wages that would have been sent to her directly. Ezi had gone over to see Kasiam as soon as she heard. Really, who went to a new family to work as a maid and asked to be allowed to take a nap before starting? Kasiam should have known better. 'Make yourself indispensable to them,' Rapu's mother had advised. And as far as Rapu was concerned there was no better time to start than now.

The kitchen shone like the day of Creation. She wondered how much work, how much cleaning it took to keep a kitchen looking like that. The thought ached her tired bones but did nothing to diminish her eagerness. There were cupboards hanging above things she hardly recognised. There was none of the simplicity of her mother's kitchen. None of the soot that caked the walls; none of that stuffy kitchen smell. This kitchen had no smell.

'Where are the pots, Aunty?' Ezi pulled open a cupboard and dragged out a pot so shiny Rapu was sure it had never been used.

'This is where you keep the pots.'

Where to start? Rapu looked up at Aunty for guidance.

'I think we should have yam porridge. Get me a tuber of yam from that pile.'

Rapu brought a tuber. Ezi opened more cupboards and pulled out a bottle of palm oil, a plastic box with ground crayfish, onions and a jar of ground pepper. No wonder this kitchen did not smell of anything. Everything was boxed or tinned and put away. Ezi opened the fridge and brought out some tomatoes and meat wrapped in layers of newspaper. Better, Rapu thought. She had begun to imagine that she was expected to cook with neither meat nor fish. The meat was not as much as she had thought people in the city ate, but still it was better than nothing. Kasiam had told her that the couple she had gone to live with cooked chunks of meat as huge as a newborn's head. Rapu was starting to think that her friend had exaggerated. Either that or these people, for all their opulence, were miserly.

Ezi equipped Rapu with a knife, a mortar and a pestle and set her to work. This was work Rapu was comfortable with. She did not particularly care for yam porridge, and certainly not yam porridge without any spinach, but she did not mind. She was already starting to feel at home. She peeled the yam, sliced it and then cubed it the way her mother had taught her to. She chopped the onion and pounded it to a paste. She sang as she worked like she would back home. She sang the same songs her mother sang while she cooked and tried not to think of her, not to wonder what she was doing at this very moment. She was now a city girl, and this was what everyone in her family wanted for her. To succeed.

The first test came when the yam was washed, the meat cut into portions and ready to be cooked. No matter how long she looked, she could not find anything that looked like it could be used. Everything glimmered. There was no wood for kindling a fire, but that did not surprise Ezi. Kasiam had told her that in the city people did not use wood because they cooked inside their homes. They cooked on a huge white box, but there was no white box in this kitchen. Things were either black or the colour of metal.

5

The first week, Rapu found herself strutting around the house like she owned it. She sat in its deep couches when nobody was around to spy on her. She ran her fingers along the wooden banisters of its stairs. She lay on the deep rug of her room. She could feel its comforting warmth, its magnificence, soak into her, and she imagined that she was engulfed in a fantastically bright light.

It was impossible for her to think of her family back home. This was home now. This house. This bed with a proper mattress that she was getting used to sleeping in. This fan that kept the heat at bay. This alarm clock that went *dring-dring-dring* in the morning to wake her up. This toilet in the bowl of which she had washed clothes (and how Aunty Ezi had laughed at her). All of this, the house in its entire opulence, was home. This was her life now and if she worked hard and stuck at it, she would make her parents enough money to build their own. Nothing on this scale, of course, their ambitions were more modest: a cement building with a zinc roof to replace their mud hut with the thatch roof that leaked every rainy season. And a foam mattress for everybody. She would ask them to give away the mats on which they slept now. Or to burn them, she did not care. She would light the bonfire herself. That is how prosperous they would be. Uncle Mike had told her father that for as long as she stayed with them, he would pay her one hundred naira every month. By her father's arrangement, fifty naira would be sent to him and the other half would go to her to buy whatever necessities she needed. She knew what she would buy with her first month's salary. It did not matter that she did not need it now. It would come in handy soon, that she was sure of, on all the good food she would be fed, for it was not by God's will that she had under-formed breasts. She knew it. It was just a matter of time and hers, too, would soon start to show.

She played with the light switch in her room, delighting in watching the bulb come on, lifting the room out of the darkness. It was surely how the first day of Creation must have felt.

In the morning, Uncle Mike left for his supermarket on the Ahmadu Bello Way where many Igbo men had their shops. He said that since the '67 war, relations had improved. *Ndi* Igbo ought to move their shops in the heart of the Hausa townships, but so far that had not happened.

His supermarket enjoyed the success that came with the rise in the minimum wage and the end of the drought which had kept people less inclined to splash money on non-essentials. He said he was rushed off his feet attending to customers who wanted this and that after the tough years they have had in Kaduna. Rapu did not understand what the minimum wage was but if it made people flock to Uncle Mike's shop, then she was happy. If it made Uncle Mike recount the stories

164

of how many customers he had served that day to her – not like a servant but like a member of the family – she was grateful too for the new minimum wage.

'I'm so tired today, is there any food for me?' he'd ask as soon as he got in, dropping his leather briefcase on the table as if the weight of it was too much for him to bear any longer. He was tired. Yet it was Aunty Ezi who spent most of her time in bed as if she were rushed off her feet tending to customers. When she was out of bed, it was only to stretch out in the sitting room and have Rapu bring her 'something cold to drink' while she watched TV or sang along to a Highlife tune. At other times, inexplicably, she knitted. There was hardly any part of the house that was not decorated with her handiwork. Purple coasters. White table-runners that didn't look quite finished. Yet she did no other work.

Really, such laziness, such indolence, was unimaginable, even if one did have a maid, Rapu thought. The mistress of the house next door cooked for her husband every single day. And she personally bathed her children before they went to bed, no matter how tired she was. Rapu was not complaining, the work was not insurmountable, but a lazy woman only left holes through which her husband could be snatched away from her. Men did not like lazy women. No man did. And Rapu sometimes saw the look in Uncle Mike's eyes when he spoke to his wife. They were filled with compassion. No, not compassion. Pity. As if he was already thinking of leaving her and was seeing into that future when she would be stranded, a woman alone. And of course no one would blame him. And he would look at her like that and then she would smile and say, 'Darling, *i na-atago*?', as if she could not quite believe that he had come home again to her. And then he would smile and kiss her on the cheek. And she would start glowing all over and then Rapu pitied her because any one with eyes could see that Uncle Mike was busy leaving her.

Sometimes, Aunty Ezi's friends came over. Women whom Rapu could never tell apart because they looked like clones of one another. Afros big enough to tip them over, sunglasses hiding their eyes and car keys dangling from their wrists. They looked like they had stepped out of a TV film, that was how glamorous they were. Sometimes the women came with their children who spoke only English and had cheeks so full and smooth, she felt the urge to pinch them. It was only when the children came that Rapu noticed the silence, the huge engulfing silence, that covered the house at other times. It was only then that she wondered why Aunty Ezi had no children.

'Maybe he used her womb for *ogwu*,' Anwuli said when Rapu mentioned it. Anwuli was the maid of the family that lived in the next compound. Their house was smaller than Uncle Mike's, and Anwuli's room doubled as the storage space for bags of rice and sacks of potato. But Anwuli had lived in the city far longer than Rapu had. Rapu disagreed. Uncle Mike was not the sort of man who would do deals with the devil for wealth. You could tell just by looking at him. 'Excessive wealth in exchange for his wife's womb? No!'

'Oh well, believe what you will. You just be careful. These people with money, you can never trust them.'

Rapu decided that Anwuli was just jealous and for a very long time she did not talk to her. They only made

166

up when Anwuli offered to help her to plait her hair. Aunty Ezi had said that if she could find no one to help her keep her hair tidy, Rapu would have to shave it off. Every bit of it. As if Aunty Ezi did not know that it was a taboo to shave a young girl's head as if she were a widow.

'I am telling you, Anwuli, that woman is a witch! Really, what the city does to people. What forgetfulness it wreaks on their memories, on their sense of propriety.'

6

Many years later, Rapu could still recall the incident of the fish head down to the smallest detail. She could feel the humiliation as if it had just happened.

On that day, Aunty Ezi's friend, Aunty Ifedi, was visiting. A woman with a frown etched like a tattoo on her face, Rapu did not like her very much. She was almost as bad as Aunty Ezi, always wanting something to eat, to drink. 'You'd think she only comes to the house to fill her belly! Doesn't she have any food in her own house? These city women have no shame,' she once complained to Anwuli.

Between them, Aunty Ifedi and Aunty Ezi kept Rapu on her feet fetching, carrying and cooking all day. This time, Aunty Ifedi had brought with her, for a change, some fresh fish and asked Rapu to make a pot of fish pepper soup. It was not even the weather for it. It was a very hot day. Rapu sweated as she descaled the fish, washed it and chopped it up into huge chunks. She tried not to breathe in the stench of it. She did not like the smell of raw fish at all, and at home her mother let her get out of cleaning it. There was more than enough fish to feed her entire family and yet those two wanted it as a mere snack. Aunty Ezi never ate fish head, and, of course, fish head was never served to the master of a house so whenever fish was on the menu, Rapu took it for herself. She thought of it as her reward for having to bear the smell, and the thought of the delicious fish head kept her going.

When the fish was ready, Rapu ladled out the head and put it aside. She emptied the rest of the fish into a dish, covered it like she had been taught and took it out to the women, spoons clattering on the tray. Back in the kitchen she sat down to her feast. She took methodical care to gouge out the eyes and put them to one side for future enjoyment. Then she started on the side of the head, eating with eyes closed, revelling in the delight of the spices bursting open in her mouth. She was proud of how well she had cooked it, how tasty it was. Fish pepper soup was touch-and-go with her. Sometimes it just did not turn out right at all. Lost in her culinary paradise, she did not see Aunty Ifedi enter the kitchen or hear her shriek her name. So when the slap came it was a total surprise.

'What happened to the fish head, you little thief?'

Thwat! And out came flying particles of half-masticated fish head.

'Where's the fish head?'

She lifted a palm to the smarting cheek and the only thing she could think of saying was 'Aunty Ifedi?', like a question. This seemed to infuriate the woman.

'Aunty Ifedi what? I gave you a whole fish to cook, what happened to the head?'

'I ate it, ma.'

'You ate what? Did I say you could eat it?'

'No, ma.' She had realised by now that it was useless trying to explain, that there was nothing to explain.

'And stand up when I am talking to you!' She stood.

She was breaking all the rules. How could she have so recklessly forgotten? If she was sent back home, then what? What would happen to her? And to her father? How would he manage while waiting for his sons to get tired of studying and find jobs? They brought home good report cards to their father who asked, bewildered, 'Is it report cards that we'll eat?' They announced that they were being considered for scholarships to learn more things. 'And how will I pay?' To which the older son once responded, 'Scholarship means you do not have to pay at all. Government will pay.'

'Nobody ever gives out anything for nothing. What will *gofment* want after you've finished? Cows? Your wives? Your lives? What?'

And the boys had no answer.

'Your brothers are fools,' he told Rapu. 'You're the only one I can depend on.'

Aunty Ifedi dragged her by one ear out to where Aunty Ezi was sitting, legs stretched out in front of her.

'Ezi, you're spoiling your maid, *eziokwu*. She ate my fish head. What guts!'

Aunty Ezi looked her up and down and when she spoke it was to ask her if anyone in her family could afford to buy such fish, to ask if she wanted to go back to the poverty she had escaped, to say she did not tolerate thieves. 'What you've done is steal. Next time you want something you ask the owner first!'

Rapu stood. The fish she had eaten was sticking in a lump in her throat refusing to dislodge, no matter how much she swallowed. She wished there was a way she could tell these women, these pompous women, that her parents might not be rich but they knew what was right and wrong – which was more than she could say for them. She wished she could tell Aunty Ezi how lazy she was, how unjustifiably lucky she was to land a man like Uncle Mike, a man who deserved a woman far, far better than the one he got. She wished she could throw her barenness in her face, sing for her the songs they sang for women whose wombs were withered in the village, to tell her that a hen that did not lay eggs was not of much use to anyone. But she did not. She could not. She stood, shuffling her legs on the rug, waiting to be discharged so that she could cry in private. She knew she had done wrong, but to be branded a thief was unbearable. Released at last, she ran to a corner of the kitchen and wept for the disgrace of her father's poverty, wept for the frustration of keeping mute. And then she swore an oath to herself.

7

Uncle Mike could never get her name right. No matter how many times Aunty Ezi corrected him (Rapu did not, of course), he never remembered. He would shout for her, a towel around his waist, to get him a glass of water from the kitchen. 'Ije! Agnes! Eunice!' and Aunty Ezi would giggle and shout, 'Rapu! Rapu!' and he'd repeat the name, even if Rapu had answered already, laughing a laughter that glinted in his eyes. And when he called her to take the glass back to the kitchen he would call her by a different name.

'Your uncle is getting holes in his head like an old man,' Aunty Ezi would tease, and husband and wife would laugh but Rapu never laughed. A woman mustn't ridicule her husband in front of another. Not even to joke. It seemed like this woman's mother did not do a very good job of teaching her manners. And Aunty Ezi could not see what Rapu saw. That even when her husband laughed, *hee hee hee ha ha ha*, he was really elsewhere.

Rapu was certain that Uncle Mike had a woman outside. All men did but wise women kept their eyes sharp and their tongues warm and they saw and they lured their men back home before things got out of control. 'Men are like palm wine,' her mother told her when she was old enough to know. 'You sip a bit at a time and you sip it with respect, otherwise you lose all sense of what is wrong and right and start to dig your own grave.' Her mother, her wise mother, could teach this woman a thing or two about holding on to her husband. Especially how to treat your man in front of another woman. No matter the size of your husband's penis, no other woman should know it. Every girl was taught that back in the village. You only showed familiarity with your husband in private. Other women should not be privy to it.

And yes, she was a woman too. Her breasts were starting to shoot out. She did not need to pinch them any more, did not need to coax them to bloom. They were doing that all by themselves now. And she had started to kill her chicken. It had come before, about a year ago when she still lived with her parents, but then, just as she was getting excited, it had stopped. And now it looked like it had come to stay. She had become a proper woman. Her hips would fill out, and her stomach too. It was too shallow in the middle, almost like a spoon. She looked undernourished with a stomach like that and she hated it, although not as much as she had hated her little breasts. When she complained to Anwuli, she had told her off for being silly and brought her stacks of magazines with pictures of girls whom she said were big models in Amayreeka, making enough money to buy the whole of Kaduna all because of the way she looked. 'All the girls here want to look like you. And you're complaining! *Chei!* You don't know how lucky you are, oo.' Rapu had looked at the pictures and seen no reason why anyone should pay the girls loads of

173

money for looking like they did, as undernourished as herself. Really, she said, she did not care whether or not these girls got money, she did not want to look like that. Secretly she doubted Anwuli's story very much. How did she know what happened in Amayreeka when she had not even been to Lagos, which, everyone agreed, was a preparation for abroad? And if that was really in vogue why did Anwuli not try to look like that herself? She had a round stomach, the perfect stomach, and that was what Rapu wanted too. And now with the onset of her period, she felt sure that it was within reach. Anwuli had shown her the right type of sanitary towels to buy (no way was she going to ask Aunty Ezi). The lucky thing was, it had started at night. She recognised the dull ache in her stomach and got the confirmation she sought when she swabbed herself with a piece of toilet paper. She made a thick pad with rolls of tissue to last her the night. The next morning, when she was sent to the market, she stopped at Anwuli's to ask for her help.

She was grateful for Anwuli really, for how difficult life would be without her. She lived off the older girl's experiences in the city and discovered the city through her. On her part, Anwuli enjoyed reliving her days as a newcomer in Kaduna and delighted in pointing things out to Rapu. She enjoyed seeing her marvel at things she, Anwuli, was already starting to take for granted. So Rapu tagged on to Anwuli's hems, soaking up everything she could, mimicking her sophisticated, successful (especially with the male traders), urban way, with your chest pulled out as far as it could go, your tone of voice lowered and eyes lifted just so.

'You let the men touch you if they want to. They'll never go overboard anyway, not in the market.' So Rapu let them hold her wrist, hold her waist and run a quick palm across her chest if no one was looking. This sort of behaviour would not have been tolerated in the village. A girl would never let a man touch her like that in public for a thousand naira. But Rapu loved this freedom, this freedom to be touched that was particular to the city. So she giggled as the men felt her and she haggled for the best bargains for bags and tops and brassieres which caught her fancy.

As soon as traders brought in new wares, Anwuli would tell Rapu, 'A togo bell, they've rung their bell.' And if Rapu could she would join her and off they would go to get lost in the shiny bright colours of ready-made clothes imported from countries they had no hope of ever going to.

8

They were having guests for dinner, some important friends of Uncle Mike's, and he wanted a banquet. *Isi ewu* and three types of rice, three kinds of soups, pounded yam and a big platter of salad. Rapu woke up early and set to work. She hoped that today Aunty Ezi would realise the enormous amount of work ahead of her and help her a little bit. Just a little bit would do. How was she expected to make all that before noon? If this were in the village her mother's friends would have been over helping to wash the rice and chop the vegetable and offering to go home with the prepared ingredients and cook. Help was always offered. Here the women only came to eat. The visitors, did they not have wives? She counted out twelve cups of rice into a wide tray and set a pot of meat on a burner to boil.

It was all right for Uncle Mike to order all this food. He was a man, and men had no sense of how much work went into cooking. They just sat and waited to be served. It was their right. She did not begrudge that. She sat on a kitchen stool, placed the tray on her knees and started picking out stones from the grains of rice. Men had no idea how tiring it was, how much energy was expended on cooking, so of course Uncle Mike could ask her to make rice and soup and salad and abacha but it was up to his wife to contain the excesses, to tell him in that voice of hers, 'Darling, it's too much food for one person to make.' And failing that, the least she could do was come and help. After all, Rapu had only one set of hands. She washed the rice, strained the chaff and set a pot on another burner. She unwrapped the two heads of goat that had been in the fridge since yesterday and washed them thoroughly. She rinsed the ears out, scrubbed the skin with a sponge and then placed each in a pot of water. Salted and spiced. It was time to start work on the sitting room.

Sometimes she felt like the mistress of the house. She had complete dominion over everything that mattered, everything that made one a wife: she cooked, she cleaned. And it was she who Uncle Mike called if he needed anything. Her mother would be proud of her. She had made herself indispensable.

She wiped the dusty glass surface of the framed wedding pictures she had been warned by Aunty Ezi to handle with care. (As if she was the one with butter-fingers who dropped drinking glasses and laughed and said, 'Oh, how very clumsy I am becoming.') She dusted carefully, starting with the large photograph leaning against the wall beside the television, two shiny faces smiling into the camera. (She had always thought it odd that they would choose to look into the camera rather than into each other's eyes, like they did in the foreign films that Aunty Ezi liked to watch. Rapu would look into her husband's eyes for their wedding portrait. That was how she had always imagined it. That was the only proper way to do it.) She traced concentric circles around Uncle Mike's face and a swish-swash across Aunty Ezi's;

177

then she carefully wiped their necks, shiny in their sweatiness (she would make sure her husband did not sweat. She would take care to wipe his neck with the white handkerchief tucked in her oh-so-petite wedding bag imported from London. His sweat would turn her scented handkerchief musky and brown but what did such things matter when compared to a husband's comfort?); then brushed over the wedding outfits. Uncle Mike's black jacket and red tie no longer straight but flayed halfway across his chest, as if it was going away for a short walk. And then she moved on to Aunty Ezi's dress with a bodice of beads that were sure to have been uncomfortable (her smile in the picture did look slightly pained. She, Rapu, with impeccable taste and good sense would ask for a simple dress of white lace and puffed sleeves to show off her full arms and her chest, which would have grown impressive, so her smile in her own wedding photograph would be the confident, easy smile of a happy bride).

She dusted the back of the photograph for cobwebs and then moved on to the centre table with the glass top which she had admired when she first arrived, but no longer thought of as beautiful. If truth be told, she found it rather ridiculous. Tables should be sturdy and made of wood, not something as brittle, as crass as glass. It almost embarrassed her that she had liked it. And it took forever to get clean, especially if a young visitor had smudged it with hands coated in chocolate. She rubbed and wiped, cursing Aunty Ezi for choosing such a table. It was heartbreaking to spend time and energy on something so completely grotesque, so un-beautiful. She would break it and replace it with something much more worthy of the opulence of the house if she could. She dusted the chair arms and rearranged the doilies on the two tables either side of the sofa.

She had once admired the doilies, finding beauty in their fragile patterns, but now they too embarrassed her. She could find no use for them, no reason for their existence. She could not vacuum the floor until Aunty Ezi and Uncle Mike woke up. She would have preferred a broom for the sitting room but Aunty Ezi had warned her never to use one on the rug. 'A broom is too harsh. It will make the threads run so.' Nothing for it but to tackle the other parts of the house while she waited.

There was still the guest toilet and the hallway to clean. The thought of all the tasks still waiting weighed heavy on her. By the time Uncle Mike, the earlier riser of the two, got up, she was back in the kitchen mixing the goat head.

'You're quite a fast worker,' he said, standing in the kitchen doorway sniffing in the combined aroma of the soups simmering on the fire.

Rapu, hands deep in the mortar mixing the dish, smiled at the compliment.

Uncle Mike came in and dipped a hand into the mortar and tried a piece of meat.

'*Osoka*. Delicious. When you serve this later, make sure you serve the specials separately. I want to show Alhaji the proper way to eat this.'

'Yes, sir.' She drew a saucer to her and fished out the specials: four eyes, four ears, two tongues and four ears. She did not like the crunchiness of the ears but she loved the eyes, the salty liquidness of them.

★   ★   ★

Aunty Ezi did not rise until close to noon when she sauntered out to inspect the food, opening pots and gazing in them as if they contained some secret written message for her. She gave Rapu instructions: which plates to use, which glasses to bring out. 'And we've run out of Guinness. You'll have to go right now for five bottles of Guinness.'

Rapu, her whole body begging respite, dragged herself out. The visitors ate and sighed in pleasure and said they had never eaten any food so rich in texture, so delicious. And when one of the men asked Aunty Ezi if it had been her handiwork, Uncle Mike smiled and said no, the honour must go to Rapu. And he shouted to her so that they could take a good look (as if they had not seen her before; she it was who had brought in the food, the spoons, the glasses and bottles of drinks). He did not falter. 'Rapu!' he shouted, and the suddenness of it and the rightness of it filled her with delight as she scuttled out of the kitchen. 'These people want to see the fantastic chef!'

They wondered aloud at her smallness, her culinary magic. They complimented her in Hausa (of which she understood very little) and in English (of which she understood even less).

'You are a splendid find,' an effusive woman with a pimpled face said in Igbo. 'I must come and borrow you for one of our parties. You will let us borrow her, won't you?' She looked at Aunty Ezi but it was Uncle Mike who said, 'Any time', as if Rapu was his to give away. Rapu beamed with happiness. She would go anywhere for Uncle Mike. And the happiness filled her head and bent it. The effusive woman laughed and said, 'What a shy creature.' And Aunty Ezi dismissed Rapu and sent her back to the kitchen to wait until she was called.

When she was, it was Aunty Ezi again. The visitors had gone and Rapu was to clear the mess they had left behind. Bones chewed and spat out at the edges of the glass centre table; oil stains from soup that had slipped off spoons and marked the white doilies; a half-eaten goat tongue that had mysteriously found its way under the table. Rapu sweated in the heat as she cleaned up but not once did she feel the ache in her bones. Not once did she come down from the clouds she had been sitting on since Uncle Mike spoke as if she belonged to him in a way a wife might belong to her husband.

Aunty Ezi asked her to hurry up. 'How long does it take to wipe a table?' But she did not mind. She hurried up. She flew. Her stomach growled from hunger but she barely heard it. Aunty Ezi had told her to serve every-thing and only eat what was left over. Like she needed reminding. She was a good maid. She knew the rules. Nobody could fault her on that. Besides, she was not even sure she had the appetite for the bit of jollof rice that was left, the lump of semovita that was sure to fill her up on any day, the *isi ewu* that had been miraculously spared for her. Under normal circumstances, she would have rejoiced in this, but these were not ordinary circumstances.

9

MIKE UGWU'S SUPERMARKET: ONE STOP FOR ALL YOUR NEEDS read the sign on the Ahmadu Bello Way, right after the Convent of the Holy Rosary Sisters. Exactly how Mike had imagined it. He took pride in ordering stock. He took pride in organising the shelves, deciding what went where: cans of milk right under the packets of sugar, which are beside the loaves of bread. He had shampoos stacked beside hair conditioners and litres of orange juice.

'It's all strategic,' he explained to Ezi once. Most people who come to buy shampoos are on their way to a hairdressing salon. Beauty salons breed thirst but people hardly think about the thirst. Once they see the juice, they remember, and they buy litres of it to see them through the day. 'It's all about strategy.' And Ezi nodded and looked with pride at her husband.

Mike plotted what to order and what not to, so that he was always one step ahead of the other supermarkets in Kaduna. He had a nose for business.

This was what he had dreamt of as soon as he was old enough to dream. He was not just successful, he was more successful than he had thought was possible. He had exceeded his ambition. But his other dream eluded him. If only he could have a child. It was not for lack of trying. He had thrown his energy into it, thrusting his seed into his wife's womb, but after four years, there was still nothing to show for his troubles. His mother told him he was an idiot for not replacing Ezi with a woman who could have babies for him. He reminded her of how taken she had been with Ezi when they met. 'Yes, but that was then,' she said. 'Four years and no child, people are starting to talk. They're starting to wonder if you are a man.'

'I don't care what people say.'

'And you don't care that you've got no baby? All the hard work, the sweat you pour into that shop of yours, who is it for? Will you carry your wealth to the grave to distribute to your ancestors? *Biko*, talk sense.'

His friends said the same.

'You don't have to kick her out. She's a wonderful woman, but you do need a child.'

'Get a girlfriend, get her pregnant and raise the baby.'

'Seek treatment. I hear Dr Maiwada is an expert on such issues.'

Mike had seen doctors, first alone and then with Ezi. They had both been prodded and poked and were forced to reveal the most intimate details of their lives. The verdict was indisputable but unhelpful – 'You are both very healthy, there's no reason why you shouldn't have a baby' – delivered with a smile which the couple suspected was supposed to calm their fears but which did the exact opposite.

When Ezi met Mike, she liked to say, she had not been looking for a husband. She was not like one of those women who measured their worth by the ease with which they snagged a man. She had had bigger plans; ambitions her parents were convinced were not desirable in a girl. An education was good, they agreed, but that came secondary to a husband. 'After all,' her mother said, 'everyone knows that girls go to university to find husbands, not to chase away men who approach them.' There was nothing stopping her from marrying and then, with her husband's blessing, continuing with her education. 'Some men like to flaunt their wives' learning even if the women do nothing with the degrees at the end of the day. To work with your diploma is not the goal,' she would remind Ezi. 'So why act like getting it is the most important thing of all? Girls nowadays are too greedy! In our day, we were happy just to serve our men. Women who went to school became nurses or teachers – professions that encouraged the virtues of nurturing and caring, the perfect professions for a wife.'

Ezi had no patience with her mother's standpoint. She enjoyed studying, found numbers fascinating and was aiming for a first-class degree in Accounting, after which she would do a masters and get a job with a top-notch firm. 'Times have changed,' she told her parents, and she for one was happily changing with the times. 'I am a pioneer,' she said. 'I am one of the few women in my department. It is up to us to encourage other women by staying on and chasing our dreams. And no, those dreams do not include marriage, at least until I have my degree firmly in my hand.'

Her mother fretted and worried and warned her that there was no reversing an old womb. 'The longer you wait,' she said, 'the slimmer the chances of having a baby when you eventually get married, *afo talu mmili atago mmili.*' To which Ezi replied, to much *tut-tut-tutting* from her mother, that she did not care at all if she never had children or if she never got married. In her third year of university she met Mike. And when she did, there was no doubt in her mind that he was the one whom she would allow to derail her well-laid plans. She liked to say it was the way he walked, drawing arcs with his heels as if marking out his property, claiming every inch of ground he stepped on. That confidence – for that surely was confidence – was a turn-on. She did not know anyone else with that sort of casual authority. Did not know anyone else who could build an empire with each step. She wanted him to claim her. To enclose his arms around her shoulders and mark her out as his. He always teased her that she liked him because she had a crush on Jackie Jackson and he was the closest she could ever get to him. But the truth was more banal. She wanted children that would look like him: his compact row of small, beautiful teeth; his broad shoulders; his long, lazy smile. She wanted to pass these on to her children.

She had dated many men. And what a variety they were. Her best friend declared that she had no type. The only thing her men had in common was the most obvious: they were male. 'And they have balls. And I do not mean that metaphorically because you've dated some shameless cowards!' And the two friends laughed at the memory of an ex-boyfriend who used Ezi as a shield on a dark night when they heard what they thought were gun shots. It turned out to be the faulty exhaust pipe of the deputy rector of the university. That same night, Ezi dumped him.

She had received – and rejected – as many marriage proposals as the men she had dated. She did not reject them all immediately but had agonised over some, lying awake at night unable to sleep because she could not say 'no', but was not convinced she should say 'yes'. With Mike, even before he'd proposed – stumbling over his words – she never doubted what her answer would be. She took pride in all her friends' milestones and quelled the little voice inside that told her she ought to be jealous. She was there for each pregnancy and helped as best she could when Amara complained of nausea, she prescribed her mother's foolproof therapy: she made her suck on a spoonful of ground coffee.

The children, on their part, loved their Aunty Ezi and screamed with excitement whenever they saw her at the doorstep, loaded, as she was wont to be, with packets of sweets and biscuits and books. They reminded her of what she did not have, but she loved them nevertheless. And Amara told her that God saw how well she loved children and was sure to bless her with her own one day. It was only a matter of time. She had to be patient about it. And yet sometimes when she watched her friends' perfect children, she looked for a flaw in them and when she spotted it – a temperamental child, for example – she rejoiced. It meant that children were not so desirable after all. She had not failed Mike, no matter what his brother and his cousin Silas and his friends said.

There was no reason why she could not have a baby. All the doctors they had seen said so. They ran tests and collected samples and swabs so intimately she felt violated but they could not grant her the one thing which crept up and haunted her dreams. The one thing Mike said he never thought about at all because they were happy the way they were: just the two of them with more money than they had ever dreamt of having.

For years his mother tried to get him to do two things: the first was to move back to the south of the country. The second was to marry another wife. She had failed in both attempts and for that she had often told Mike that he was a stubborn son, an obstinate son who deserved nothing good. And he told her in reply that he already had everything good, that nothing could add to the joy, to the fulfilment of being with a woman he loved in a city he loved. And, as he told Silas once, these were not just empty words. Silas had laughed and said he thought Ezi had slipped something in his water, some powerful love juju, because nobody but a man possessed would talk like that. 'You don't care that nothing will be left of your immediate family when you go?'

'Egbuna's wife is ensuring that the family name lives on. She pops out a son every year.'

'That's Egbuna's family, Egbuna's children. What of Mike's? You love Ezi, but that doesn't mean you cannot marry a second wife.'

'That's where we differ, Silas. I cannot separate sex and love. And I'll not get a wife just so she can give me a baby. Besides, God will give us a baby in His good time.'

'In God's good time! In God's time! That's a lazy man's consolation. Ever heard of the saying that God only helps those who help themselves? *Nwoke m i bukwa mmadu?*'

And so the argument went with his mother and with

Silas, leaving his family and friends convinced that he was not altogether sane, increasing their new-found suspicion and dislike of Ezi.

It was this weight that made Ezi so lethargic that she could no longer run her household, made her certain that unless she got a maid, she would go insane. Amara had told her about a TV show in which a pastor said that very often what barren women needed to open their wombs was to take in someone young to look after them. And so she asked Mike to get her a young girl, young enough to be her daughter, to help her around the house and ease the loneliness when he was at work. Someone the angels would see her taking care of and loving and so bear her silent prayers to God themselves. But she had not counted on love like that not being a given.

If anyone had asked her, she would have said she had the capacity to love anyone. Anyone. And yet even before she had a reason, she found herself disliking Rapu. And she tried. She did try. It wasn't anything the girl had done. Worse, it wasn't anything she had not done. Maybe it was her eagerness to please, her pre-empting Mike's wishes, seeing how she pleased her husband when she brought him a glass of water even before he realised he was thirsty. Hearing Mike say, 'What would I do without you?' Plus the girl was growing. No longer the spindly-legged waif they had brought back from Lokpanta, she was filling out. Come on, she told herself, don't be silly. You can't be jealous of a maid. She had thought of sending her to school or to learn a trade so that she was not in her face all day long, but Rapu had resisted. 'Aunty Ezi, really I have no head for school. And as for trade, I'm learning all I need to learn here.' She could not insist when the girl was so against it. Amara had suggested several times that maybe Ezi find a career. 'You have a degree, *nwanyi a*. You can easily pick up a job if you don't like staying at home so much.'

True, she had the qualifications and true, she could most probably find a job very easily but Mike would not let her. She had broached the subject tentatively in the first month of their marriage and Mike had looked at her with a sad smile as if she had hurt him.

'Is there anything you need I'm not giving you?'

'It's not about that.'

'Then what is it about? Have you ever had to ask for anything? Have you ever gone hungry for one day in this house? You're my woman. My wife. It's my duty to work and provide for us, and yours to look after us.'

She did not have the stomach to fight with this man whom she loved so very, very much. So she kept silent. And silence was definitely acquiescence. And the matter was never raised again. She stilled her restlessness, but instead of disappearing, it transformed itself into a lethargy of mind and body so debilitating that some mornings she had trouble getting out of bed. And now she had Rapu, she did not need to get out at all. She could have every wish granted from the luxury of her bedroom.

'Rapu, prepare lunch.'

'Rapu, do some laundry.'

'Rapu, get me a glass of water.'

'Rapu, we've run out of Omo, go to Uncle's super-market and get a box.'

'Rapu, bring me an orange. No, make that two.'

Rapu worked with a precision and an efficiency that irked Ezi. The girl seemed almost perfect, the ideal maid. She knew her friends envied her. They all complained of their maids. They stole, they were indolent, and they were terrible cooks. There was nothing to criticise in Rapu and so Ezi magnified her little flaws to justify her exaggerated reactions to them. She wished she had never asked for help. She chided herself often for giving in to this illogical dislike, hatred even. Illogical jealousy of a girl without an education. How could she for one moment think Rapu was a threat to her, that Mike would look at Rapu as anything other than a maid? She tried to laugh away her fears and kept Rapu on her toes. How her friends would mock her if they heard. And Mike. Mike, if he suspected, would be insulted. He would probably say, 'You think I'm a dog?' She wanted to confess to Mike so that he would tell her that and allay the worry that was niggling at the edges of her mind but she feared his scorn even more. So she kept quiet and at night she held on tight to Mike's back and gave him kisses that made him sigh. She had nothing to fear. Still, one heard stories of lusty men and their wayward maids. But not Mike. Certainly not Mike. She could, of course, send Rapu back to her parents but what reason would she give? What could she invent? Even the blind could see how well the girl worked. How could she, who nagged Mike into getting her help (and she did need help), after less than a year tell him that she had changed her mind? No, that was no option. Nevertheless, she watched Rapu with hawk's eyes. Watchfulness was her guard word. Watchfulness and alertness.

But sometimes, it is not the thing that we fear most that crushes us but that which we have forgotten to fear. It is that which we have forgotten that slithers in under the door. These were the words her friend Amara would tell Ezi when, a few months later, Ezi called to tell her that her world was falling apart.

10

Now they battled the Kaduna harmattan. Rapu, unprepared for such bitter weather, did not know how to tackle it. Her lips chapped and the cold callused her hands. Aunty Ezi watched how Rapu's youthful beauty was marred by the weather. She delighted in it. And when she called Rapu every night into the bedroom to rub okwuma into her soles, she rejoiced in the girl's palms, like sandpaper, smoothing the shea-butter lotion into her legs.

Rapu had heard that the north could get cold but she had never anticipated this. She giggled when Uncle Mike told her that America was even colder, that it was as cold as a freezer. At night she covered herself in her mother's wrapper, which had lost its smell of home, and in the mornings she tied the wrapper around her to cover the transparency of the cotton nightgown she had inherited from Aunty Ezi. Ezi's lethargy grew by the day. It took a long time for her to notice the changes going on in her own body. Rapu told her one night, 'Aunty Ezi, your ankles feel swollen.'

She tried to still the excitement rising in her as she thought back to her last period. Could it be? She dared not think it. Yes, she had taken a child in but she had not loved the girl. Could it be that Rapu had opened her womb like the pastor had promised? If it was so, she promised God, if she was really pregnant, she would love Rapu. She would force herself to treat her like she would her own child. She would never harbour one bad thought, not a single one, towards her.

The next day as soon as Mike left for his supermarket, Ezi went to see a doctor for confirmation. She collapsed when she returned home for the happiness was too much for her legs to bear. She touched her stomach under her blouse. It felt warm and throbbing with life. Something, someone, was definitely growing in there. She could feel it, and the feeling suffused her so that she felt as if she was floating. Her life would be perfect. She would give Mike a son, shut up his entire family once and for all. Oh, that insufferable Silas would be forced to swallow his words. She let out a whoop and did a jig around the room. Nothing could go wrong now. She would love Rapu, love her with a mother's love, and when her baby came, of course, she would love him too. And names, all the names she would pour on him to show him how much he was wanted, how much he meant to her. She would have a son after years of waiting, of hoping, that was what she deserved. A girl would be nice as a second child. But first a son, to provide Mike with an heir, and then a daughter to mother, the way girls needed to be. She thought of all those years of bumping into old friends when they always seemed to be searching for children hiding behind her, running between her knees, and eventually the old friend would ask, 'So, how many children have you got now? An entire football team?' And then the pained silence that preceded the declaration, 'We don't have any yet.' 'Oh,' the friend would say, 'God's time is the best.' And she had waited for that time and now, when she was least expecting it, it was here. Happy seemed so inadequate. She was not just happy, there was something else, better, higher than happy.

When Mike came back that evening, she dragged him to the bedroom and whispered the news into his ears. 'We are pregnant,' she said, and his frown became a smile. He hugged her and then drew away from her and in his face was something inscrutable but she did not give it a second's thought. The news she had just given him was overwhelming. It was a gift they had yearned for and had given up hope of receiving. Now it was here, they needed time to get used to it. They would not talk about this, not yet, because there were always things unseen and unheard by humans, ready to snatch your happiness away and crush it underfoot just for fun. They guarded the news jealously, quietly, until it began to show, and to deny it no longer made sense, but even then they did not talk about it.

Nobody spoke loudly about a pregnancy for fear of attracting the evil eye. Ezi sought other ways to communicate her impatience, her restless excitement, and so she turned to knitting more than ever before. Mike could hear her when he slept, knitting things. Little things. Baby things in woolly rainbow colours. Cardigans and socks and booties. Table coasters and multicoloured cases for sunglasses. Everywhere he looked, Ezi's handiwork was there. They leapt at him from underneath the red cushions of the sitting-room sofa. They stared at him from the top of the fridge in the kitchen; from the glass top of the table in the living room; from the bedroom dresser. And on the living-room floor, balls of wool unravelled and wound themselves around the legs of chairs like loosely held secrets. Sometimes the knitting pins click-clicking kept him awake. Mostly he did not mind. He knew it was Ezi's way of talking to him, of telling him the one thing they could not tell each other. And so she hummed and knitted and he lay face-up in bed smiling into the room. When she got tired, she sighed and heaved herself off the sofa and embraced him.

Sometimes he watched Rapu massaging her feet, rubbing her toes tenderly with the shea butter – she could no longer stand the smell but he knew she very much needed its soothing calmness.

At night she lay in the crook of his arms, breathed into his nose and was certain that life could only get better. And the gods who watched over her did cart-wheels and laughed.

11

In the dry season, Rapu often slept in only her wrapper. She woke up early and did her morning chores in her wrapper. Before the others woke up, she would already be washed and dressed. With her pregnancy, Aunty Ezi became more demanding. Rapu's work doubled. She often had to cook several times a day to cater to her mistress's cravings. Still, she cooked, washed and ran errands in her usual punctilious manner. She was looking forward to her holidays. Uncle Mike had promised her a lift home in two months' time, to Lokpanta, when he would be driving down to visit his family. Rapu was keen to go, to show off her new urban look to her friends and brothers. She was cultivating a neat afro and her wardrobe had grown immensely, thanks to her bargain hunting with Anwuli. She had three pairs of shoes with moderate heels which went *klik-klak-klik* when she wore them to church. Her Igbo, too, had been refined and polished so that she sounded more like Aunty Ezi than she did on her previous visit. They would not recognise her at all. And her breasts. Her breasts. Those excited her the most. She had seen them grow and fill a bra so that she no longer felt envious of Anwuli. She had transformed completely. But what was the use of all that transformation if there was no one to show off to? So she counted down the days and kept herself busy in the house.

She had taken her mother's advice seriously and was quite certain that she had become indispensable. She knew the house like the inside of her palm, even better than the owners themselves, she told Anwuli. And Anwuli laughed and told her that maybe one day she would become the mistress of the house and all that knowledge would come in handy. And the two girls threw their legs in the air and laughed at the ridiculousness of it. And Rapu said when she became mistress of the house, she would have Aunty Ezi out of her bed very early to train her out of her laziness. And the two girls laughed again. Their voices held no malice, no promise, just the sheer delight of two young women entertaining themselves with fantasy. That was safe. And so in the safety of impossibility (how could the tables ever turn, eh?) they invented crueller punishments for Ezi, culminating in Rapu asking Mike to expel her from the house. And Mike, of course, would do that. *Ka Ka Kaw. Ha ha ha!* Bent over in stitches and stitches of raucous laughter. But what happened was not planned.

Rapu, worn out from the night before, had woken later than usual. But the house was quiet. Aunty Ezi and Uncle Mike were still sleeping. She hurried to do her duties so that she would be dressed before they got out of bed. Somehow, as she was dusting the TV, her wrapper came loose. She let out a gasp, grabbed it and covered herself. She looked around to make sure no one had woken up and seen her. The one thing that frustrated her about the house was that it was easy to sneak up on people: the rug swallowed every footstep.

Uncle Mike lay beside Ezi and tried to shake off the image he had just seen. A wrapper falling off and allowing him a peek — a short peek because he had beaten a hasty retreat back into his bedroom, but a peek nevertheless — of Rapu's lush womanhood. Buttocks rounded like clay pots. A back that made him shiver. He had wanted to catch the early-morning news on the radio in the sitting room but now he no longer thought of the news. He could not get those buttocks out of his head. They looked perfectly moulded. He had never thought of Rapu in that way. Not as a woman, a proper woman. He had to stop this, he told himself, trying in vain to banish the picture that came into his mind. After all, he could not do anything about it. What could he do? Become one of those men who ordered their house girls into sex with them? He had more respect for his wife and for Rapu. Had he not resisted his mother's attempts to get him to take a second wife. 'You don't even have to love her. Just get her to give you a baby.'

And had he not been affronted by his mother's easy suggestion? Had he not stood by his wife? So why now was a mere slip of a girl getting him all excited? A girl young enough to be his own daughter. He wondered what her buttocks felt like, how he could knead them under his palms. The image stayed with him and prompted impure thoughts so that he found it difficult to concentrate.

Every day after that was a trial, a struggle, with temptation eating him up so that his hands shook when he accepted a glass of water from Rapu. And when he lay in bed at night beside his wife, those youthful buttocks called to him and kept him tossing and turning so that Ezi asked him if he was coming down with malaria. 'I don't think so,' he said and tried hard to lie still. Maybe he could find a reason to send the girl back to her parents, excise the temptation. But what reason would he give? Ezi had asked for the help and it was her duty to fire her. Besides, Rapu had given him no reason he could present to his wife to justify why she should be fired. It would rouse Ezi's suspicion if he were suddenly to get so involved as to suggest that the maid be fired. Besides, it would not be fair to punish the girl for nothing. It was up to him to steer his thoughts away from the danger zone they were insistent on entering.

Every day when he saw Rapu, no matter what she wore, he pictured the wrapper falling. And so perhaps it was inevitable that on the day his wife was away at a friend's wedding, he found himself, quite against his will, going to Rapu's room. And for a moment as he stood in the middle of the room, facing her as she wondered what he wanted, he felt foolish. But the moment passed.

And it seemed like destiny when she did not fight him, but opened up warmly to welcome him, as if she had waited her entire life for this. And she held him between her thighs as if she had done this many times and her tightness confused him because he could not believe that she was a virgin. And the fact that she was both saddened and exhilarated him as if he had stolen something quite precious, but had received an incredible gift at the same time. It was a burden to carry. He got out of her bed and went to take a shower. He could not believe he had gone and done it, joined the rank of men whom he despised. How could he live with himself after this? And more importantly, how could he live with Ezi? But what chance did any man, any full-blooded man with a penis between his legs, have with such a girl living in his house? Once he had seen her naked, there was no going back. The image haunted him and would have driven him mad.

He had resisted for so long, not many men would. And what had he done that was so bad that he had to lose sleep over it? He was no worse than his friends. No better, but surely no worse. Why, some of the things they got up to – sleeping with their daughters' friends, and all what-not. That had to be worse. And Ezi would never find out. He was sure Rapu understood it was their little secret. And it would never happen again. Just that one slip. But the experience was beautiful. Such tightness, such strength in one so young and lithe. He sighed again, just thinking of it. But it could not, would not, happen again. He had had his one moment of failure and that was enough. He did not want to hurt Ezi. And oh, she would be hurt, but she would not know. Rapu wouldn't say anything. And if she did, it would be her word against his. But he did not need this complication in his life. Not now. Not with the rumours that flew around. Why had he allowed this to happen? But he was just a man. He had always thought he was a better man than that. He was. He had to be. It would never happen again. How could he live in the same house with both Ezi and Rapu and pretend nothing had happened? He had taken her virginity, for goodness' sake. That was sure to be a big deal to Rapu. A girl did not surrender her virginity to her master every day.

What if she told Ezi? Well, he could always deny it, couldn't he?

That young girl was sweet. It was true what they said: you stick to the same menu for a long time, you'd go crazy over something new. But what to do? What to do? Would she tell? Wouldn't she? Had he done a really terrible thing? Or had he just succumbed to his male nature? And why had she not fought him? Why, on the contrary, had she welcomed it, encouraged it, even?

Those questions whirled around in his mind but they did not stop him from falling into a long, fulfilled sleep. The dreamless sleep of the guiltless, of the just.

Rapu always knew that whatever the gods had fated, they found a way to bring to pass. That was the greatest lesson her father ever taught her, and her father was a wise man. Everything was preordained. Seeing Uncle Mike in her room, his eyes looking like those of a man who had not slept in many days, she knew where her destiny lay. If he had not touched her, she might have made the first move. Maybe reached out and touched his beard. She was glad when he did. When he held her buttocks she knew what was expected of her and so she led him to her bed. She had thought her excitement would lift her off the earth and fly her across the room. He lifted her dress and closed his mouth around her nipple, first one and then the other, and spread her legs to carry the weight of him. And he was not heavy. He nestled between her legs and squeezed her breasts and lifted his face so that she could remove his singlet and they could lie chest on chest and he slid down and kissed her navel and she shivered and he shivered and came back up again and she felt his essence growing and throbbing and growing and she wanted to touch it and she reached down and he slid out of his trousers and she held it in her palm and it was warm and alive and he said no, and his voice sounded different as if he was dying and she spread her legs and he found the space he wanted between there and inserted himself into her and then they groaned together and it hurt for an instant and then it stopped and he came in and out and in and out and she forgot who she was, where she was and she shouted *choyooo*, for that was what she always shouted when happiness became too much for her, too much for mere words, and the sound filled her mouth and her ears and she floated and then he collapsed on her sweaty and smelling of a smell she could hear, it was that strong.

She could not sleep. All night she smelt him. And when she eventually slept, it was a sleep filled with dreams of babies who looked like Mike and of a house that belonged to her. In her bed, they had become one and she knew that nothing would separate them now. And she had not even tried to seduce him. She had not plastered her face with powder and eyeshadow like Anwuli did to get Sunday the photographer to notice her. She held her pillow to her breasts and imagined she could feel Mike's bristles as he suckled on them. She felt warm all over just thinking of it, remembering it. She grunted and smiled. Wait until she told Anwuli. But could she trust her with such a big thing? And how long must it remain a secret? Mike (he was no longer Uncle) and she were destined to be together, and sooner or later everyone would know it. And she would give him the children that he wanted. Every man needed a son. She might be young and inexperienced, but that much she knew. If she gave him a son, her future would be secured.

Rapu watched Mike, to detect signs of her elevation in his mind. He was his usual old self – forgetting her name sometimes and treating Ezi like she was a queen. If Rapu was disappointed she did not show it. On Sundays Ezi and Mike went picnicking and Rapu made and packed the sandwiches they took along. Saturday morning, they had breakfast in bed and Rapu served them. Once she spat in the egg she was frying them because she was powerless to do anything else. The week Ezi visited family she expected him to come again, she waited for him to come, willed it even, but Mike left the house early in the morning and did not come back until very late. It was as though he were avoiding being in the same house as her. She sobbed into her pillow. This sort of rejection was worse than death. A man who took your virginity was supposed to desire you so much that he thought of nothing else. It was the most precious gift you could give a man. That was what Anwuli told her. She had told her friend what had happened, but not who the man was (and had not told her she was wrong when she jumped on the possibility of it being the gateman. As if she would give herself to that skinny man with wrinkled skin!). She cried and could not share her sorrow with Anwuli whose words of stinging wisdom she was not sure she could endure just yet.

Maybe she had been too eager, too willing to give herself, and he had lost interest. Anwuli always said that only cheap girls gave in easily. The good girls said 'no' when they meant 'yes' and struggled even as they parted their legs. Never appear too eager, she had lectured while chewing, *kai kai kai*, on a piece of gum. But how could one not be eager with someone one wanted so desperately? And how did you know how to find the balance between too eager and not interested? The questions and doubts eddied in her through the sleepless nights.

On the third night of their time alone, the day before Ezi was to return, Mike came into her room. She thought she had conjured him up. She must have. He reeked of liquor and slurred when he called her name but she did not mind. She let him take her. So began a pattern whenever Ezi was out of town. She worried that Mike would not come and then just as she was giving up, he would arrive, drunk and wheezing her name. She would taste the liquor on his skin and become as intoxicated as he was.

And it was becoming more and more difficult for her to hand him over (for so she had begun to think of it) to Ezi whenever she returned. And she was tempted to tell her what was going on. In the end, her finding out was not the worst thing to happen to them. But that was all still blissfully in the future.

Soon, Ezi began to joke that Rapu was mirroring her pregnancy. 'Your ankles seem to be swelling too,' she teased the girl, and Rapu laughed. And Ezi laughed. Because really the idea of Rapu pregnant was unthinkable. The girl hardly went anywhere, so how would it happen? Plus, she was much too young. Girls her age did not keep lovers. And if they did, would not know how to keep them hidden from adult eyes.

Ezi told her friends about Rapu also starting to look pregnant. Unlike her reaction, they looked serious. They planted the seeds of doubt. How naive could she be? Did she not know that these days girls started becoming sexually active younger and younger? Why, Amara's friend's maid was only twelve when she became pregnant! 'All these girls from the villages, they get carried away by city life and spread their legs for the first man that promises them a slice of it!'

She had not really expected the girl to be pregnant. The accusation had been so ridiculous that Ezi had at first only laughed. Laughed until her stomach hurt, then she clutched her stomach and began to heave in anger.

Rapu did not want to undress when Aunty Ezi asked her to. Why should she? What sort of a woman stood over another woman and asked them to remove their clothes while they watched? So when she was asked she said, 'No.' After all, what power did this woman have that she did not have? They were both sleeping with the man, with the boss of the house, and so whatever line there was before them which placed one higher than the other had been erased.

'What did you say?'

'No. I'm not undressing.'

Thwat! A slap landed on Rapu's right cheek and she raised a palm and covered the cheek and felt it quiver under her hand.

'How dare you talk to me like that? I can see that you're growing wings, *okwa ya*? May bedbugs eat out your brain. Now before I count to three I want you to remove everything you are wearing!'

And in her eyes something shone bright and dangerous and convinced Rapu to do as her mistress asked. She had never seen the woman look this mad, as if she was possessed by some demon.

So she undressed, laying her clothes in a pile at her feet. If she died before Aunty Ezi, she would come back as a ghost and make her pay for this humiliation. She would not be wicked and kill her. She would simply torture her until she begged her forgiveness. What sort of woman made another woman undress in her presence? That was the mother of all humiliations. She would show her if she became a ghost. The only way Aunty Ezi would escape her wrath would be to die before her.

'See your stomach! You are pregnant! You dirty little thing, you tart! You're pregnant!'

Rapu said nothing. She was pregnant, and so? It was better this way, better out in the open, so that Aunty Ezi knew that they were now equal. Both carrying babies for the same man. Better out now so that they both knew where they stood. Their children would be siblings, they would share the same blood, the same father. She, Rapu, would have a child who would also call this paradise a home. Which made her what? It elevated her above a mere maid, for she could not be that any more. And if, God willing, she had a son? She would still do all the work around the house, for she was the younger of the two and not married to Mike, but she would be doing them now as an almost co-wife, as a junior wife, as a member of the family.

'Yes, ma, I'm pregnant!'

She had not meant for it to come out as a defiance, but simply as an affirmation of the older woman's shrieked statement. By the time Mike came back from work that evening, Ezi had Rapu's bag. She had asked the girl several times to name the father of her baby. 'Is it Hassan the mechanic? Haruna the shopkeeper? Who?'

Silence.

Rapu would not say a word. She carried a smile on her face and this annoyed Ezi so much that she slapped her again – *thwat!* – right across the cheek. 'So you think you're a big woman now, eh? You're pregnant and you have the guts to smile while I question you? I shall slap that smile off your face. *Kitikpa lacha kwa gi imi!* By the time I'm done with you, your parents will no longer recognise you. *Ashawo!* Whore!'

It did not take her long to decide that Rapu had to go. There was nothing else for it. She would have to leave first thing in the morning because the house was not big enough for two madams. She told Mike this as soon as he stepped into the door. 'That girl you brought for me has to leave before I kill her.'

'What has she done?'

'What hasn't she done? She's been sleeping with every penis around here. She's pregnant! And she'd better go home and have her bastard child because she won't tell me who the father is. And I'm not prepared to wait on my house girl.'

'You're sure she's pregnant?'

'Yes. I suspected and she's not even denying it.'

'In that case she has to go. I don't suppose she'll be much help here if she's pregnant.'

And so it was settled. Early the next morning, Mike took Rapu to the bus stop on his way to work. By evening she would be back in the village.

Ezi had expected to see tears of remorse and a plea for forgiveness – she got neither. When she told Amara, Amara said that she had spoilt Rapu. You keep house girls on a leash or they turn round and bite you. *I na-egekwa m nti?*'

Everybody agreed that, all round, it was good that Rapu had gone, that it was an awful thing she did getting pregnant at her age, and that it would be difficult for Ezi to cope alone with a baby on the way. Ezi's friends took turns lending her their maids until she found someone permanent: a widow from Jos who took over, mothering Ezi to the point of suffocation and infecting her with the way she doubled words. Yet it was a small price to pay for having help around the house.

It would be another six months before Rapu returned.

12

In fact, it would be wrong to say that Rapu returned. The more truthful thing to say would be that she was returned, triumphantly, by Ezi's mother-in-law, cradling a baby in her arms. The baby was bundled up in a blanket and Ezi's first thought was how very much the blanket looked like her Mma's, specially ordered from London by Mike. Mma was three months old then, a chubby child who demanded constant attention, draining both Ezi and her mother who had come to help out. Mma and her grandmother were in the guest room sleeping, and Ezi was resting in the sitting room when the doorbell went. It was she who opened the front door to her mother-in-law and a filled-out Rapu carrying a bundle in her arms. Her mother-in-law had come only twice to visit her new grandchild, saying she did not want to get in the way of Ezi's mother, who busied herself with Mma. And now here she was with the maid who had been sent home in disgrace. For a minute, Ezi thought she was in a dream.

'Good afternoon, Mama,' Ezi said, ignoring Rapu. 'Mike is not home.'

'He is now,' she said, and Ezi realised that someone else had walked up to the door. It was Mike. He looked confused for a moment, as if he had come to the wrong house. And then said the single word that crumbled Ezi's life: 'Sorry.'

Ezi understood immediately what it was for. She could see it in the smile on Rapu's face.

Every man deserved a son. If Rapu had not given him one, there was no way she would have been allowed back in. And if Ezi wanted, as soon as Rapu's son was old enough, Rapu would be sent back to the village and Ezi would never have to see her again. Mike's son had to grow up in the city. His children had to grow up together. Ezi heard Mike's pleas in bits and pieces. He had run after her when she fled into the bedroom screaming and tried to calm her down. 'It meant nothing!' Ezi could only hear the rush of her own tears. She wanted her mother. She wanted her baby, her Mma-Mma. She opened the door. Mike tried to hold her but she slapped off his hand and stumbled to the guest room. Rapu's humming could be heard from the sitting room.

'What's wrong?' her mother asked, taking in her tears, her crazed look.

And when Ezi told her, told of her world ending, her mother held her and said simply, 'There is nothing the eyes would see that would ever make them bleed. You hear me? *O nwero ife anya fulu gbaa mme.* You scared me! I thought someone had died.'

She held her daughter and let her cry. '*Ndo. Ndo.* Don't cry. Your daughter needs you. *Ndo.* Stop.'

'I wish I was dead,' Mma snorted through her tears.

'No, no. Don't ever say that. Do not invoke death by careless words. Of course you're hurt. I understand that. But that's no reason to call death upon yourself, my daughter.'

'Mama! He slept with Rapu, Mama! Rapu my maid!'

'Yes. He's betrayed you. Stop. *O zugo.*'

'And she has his baby!'

'His son! His son! And that, my dear, makes all the difference. You do not want to anger him, ooo; do not anger him because at this moment you're standing only with one leg inside the house. This Rapu has landed on both feet. You're upset now. You're angry but, my dear, after the anger, you'll have to think of how to hang on to him.'

Ezi wriggled out of her mother's embrace. Her mother might have accepted that behaviour from her own husband but she was a modern woman. Times had moved on.

'Hang on to him? I'm leaving him. There's no way I can stay.'

Her mother laughed. 'Leaving him to go where? *Ebe ka-i na-aga?* That's the problem with you girls with too much book knowledge. Where will you go with a baby this young?'

'I can. I can come back and live at home for a while until I find my feet again. I can get a job.'

'But where is home? This, here, this is home. Do not make a laughing stock of us, please. And your father suffers from high blood pressure. You want to exacerbate that? Here, the baby needs feeding. Sit down, feed her and do not say things now that you might later regret. I know how you feel, but the hurt goes away. Believe me, I know. Have you forgotten Indy?'

And it was only then that Ezi noticed that her baby, her beautiful new baby, was crying, her face all scrunched up like an old paper bag and her fists balled as if she was preparing to enter a boxing ring. No one else mattered

211

but her baby. This child that she and Mike had looked forward to and had doted upon since her birth. It had not turned out to be a boy like she had hoped, but she had realised the moment that she laid eyes on her, it had not mattered at all. 'She's as beautiful as her mother,' Mike had said. And yet all that while, he had known he was expecting another child. Mma's crying became frenzied and Ezi felt a wave of nausea. She handed the baby back to her mother and threw up all over the floor.

'Look at you,' her mother said. 'Look at you acting as if the world has ended. Your baby is hungry and you're here feeling sorry for yourself.' She hissed and went out, coming back a few minutes later with sand, which she poured over the vomit, and a glass of water for Ezi. 'You want your baby to die of starvation?'

Ezi picked up Mma, raised her blouse and started nursing the baby. Mma, oblivious to her mother's shattering world suckled greedily, pulling on the nipple as if in revenge for a meal long denied.

Everything seemed surreal. She felt detached. From the baby pulling at her nipples. From her mother scooping up the vomit from the tiles. From the sounds of another baby crying in the sitting room. This could not be happening. Not to her. Not to Mike and her. They were too solid for that. And since when did Mike believe that girls did not count? That only male children counted? That was not the Mike who had wooed her, who stood by her through the years of her childlessness. He would not do this now when their family was starting to expand. What did he need a son for when they had their own daughter?

13

How could he have thought that sending Rapu away would 'solve the problem'? This baby was not just a problem. It was not something that could be fixed. 'You betrayed me! It doesn't matter whether she's here or in Timbuktu, you have still betrayed me!'

She accused Mike of having plotted it. He was, was he not, a careful strategist, planning every move, shaking it and dusting it to make sure it was perfect? 'That's who you are! It's what you are!' That was the secret to his success as the owner of the best-known, most profitable supermarket on a street full of supermarkets.

'How could I have planned it? You were the one who wanted a house girl. How could I now be blamed for plotting it?'

Ezi clapped her hands over her ears and stomped off into the guest room.

'I can't forgive you,' she told Mike truthfully when he tried to talk to her that night, explaining that if Rapu stayed, it would only be as their maid. He would never sleep with her again. He wet his forefinger and pointed it to heaven, swearing an oath of allegiance to his wife. He was very sorry for what he had done, he said.

'Too late! You should have thought of that before you

jumped into bed with her. When I close my eyes, all I see is the two of you!'

'I am sorry. I don't know what else to do. Please, Ezi. Please.' He tried to hold her hand but she snatched it away.

'I can't forgive him,' she told her mother the next day, as she put a bag together with her clothes and her baby's. 'I can't stop imagining him with her.'

'You can make yourself forget. Just try! Don't let that little girl win!'

'It's not a contest, Mama. And I can't forget. How do I forget? Tell me.' She did not even need to close her eyes to see legs and hands tangled in her bed. She spat into a handkerchief.

'There is nothing the eyes will see that will force it to bleed. No matter how long you cry, it's tears you'll shed and not blood, so don't tell me you can't forget. You can make yourself forget anything you want to.'

'I can't forgive him. If I can't forgive, how can I forget?'

'Nobody is asking you to forgive. Acceptance and forgiveness are not the same thing. Do not conflate them, my daughter. Forgiveness cannot be forced. It comes from within us. But you can accept what has happened, for your sake, for your daughter's sake, for all our sakes! And you can make yourself forget.'

Ezi looked at her mother as if she had never seen her before and said quietly, 'No.'

Greed. Her mother said that was Ezi's biggest problem. Greed and selfishness. Not caring what it meant for her parents if she stepped out of a marriage.

Mike sent for Ezi's friends to try to persuade her to

stay. The women asked her to think about it. Would she rather be a single mother or share a husband? They knew what they would choose. Amara told her, 'Finally the baby you wanted is here. Are you going to deprive her of a father?'

Ezi, convinced by her friends, unpacked the bags she had made but stayed cooped up in the guest room with her mother who treated her like an egg, careful not to let her crack.

'The pain will go away,' her mother promised her. 'You've made a wise decision. You'll have more babies with Mike. You'll give him a son! As for that Rapu. Biting off the finger that fed her, it's good that you will not let her grow fat on that finger. Does she think she can usurp you in your own home?'

On the fourth day after Rapu's arrival, Ezi made up her mind. The situation was unbearable. 'I can't live like this, Mama. I can't sleep another night in the same house as Mike.' She had moved back to her bedroom but did not tell her mother that whenever Mike tried to touch her she was assaulted by the image of him and Rapu. There was no forgetting it, no matter how hard she tried. Nor did she tell her mother that one night when Mike's hand strayed to her thighs, she had slapped it so hard he shook it as if it burned.

Her mother warned her, 'If you leave, if you walk out of your marriage, you're not welcome at home.'

'I'll take that risk.'

'And what about Mma?'

'We'll be fine, I have a degree, after all. I can get a job. Easy!'

'It is the obstinate fly that follows a corpse to the

215

grave. I've said my piece. You want to kill yourself, go ahead!'

She feared that if she stayed any longer, she would do something terrible or have something more terrible done to her. Every time she heard Rapu's baby cry, she wanted to strangle it, to choke it, to kill the thing that had changed their lives. How could she live under the same roof as it? And even if the baby was not there physically, it would always haunt her. Either way, she could no longer stay with Mike.

And how difficult really would it be to live on her own with a baby? Things must have changed since her mother's time, when women were terrified of living alone. Society had become more intelligent, more tolerant, surely. There was no need for her to stay on in a marriage that no longer suited her just so that she could lay claim to a husband. As for Mma not having a father, she would be enough parent for two, she had enough love for two. She would make sure her daughter did not miss anything.

'Mother, times have changed,' she told her mother softly. 'Have they?' her mother scoffed and, hissing, went to bed.

The next day, Ezi's mother asked Mike to give her a ride to the bus stop. Her job here was done. She would not say goodbye to her daughter and did not say goodbye to Mma for fear of bursting into tears. The next time Ezi saw her, visiting with Mma, raising her parents' hopes that she had changed her mind, she cursed Ezi. The day her mother left, Ezi left. Without a forwarding address. Small enough not to get lost in, and familiar, Enugu seemed like a nice place to start again, to sever all ties with her past. A chance meeting at a boutique less than a year later brought her face to face again with Amara, her best friend.

'They call me Madam Gold now,' Amara told her. 'I sell all manner of gold jewellery.'

And there, in the middle of the boutique, Madam Gold and Ezi had hugged and cried like two little girls.

14

Rapu settled in quicker than she had expected. Ezi leaving was a blessing. She would not have minded sharing Mike, had expected to, had even prepared herself to defer to Ezi as the senior wife, but without any prompting, Ezi had made way for her.

Mike paid Rapu's bride price. There was nothing else to do. And so now, not only was she, Rapu, mother of the first son, but also mistress of the house. Anwuli's eyes nearly popped out the first time she came to visit. Rapu told her she was looking for a girl to help her look after the house. 'With a new baby, it's too much for me.'

'Hm, you are very lucky, oo,' Anwuli said, eyeing Rapu's new clothes, unsure now how to talk to her friend, newly promoted from maid to wife. Rapu knew it too. Her relationship with Anwuli had to be reassessed, but she had no other friends, nobody she could tell her fears and show off her happiness to.

Her mother had come to stay for a month soon after Ezi left. The bride price had been paid so that she could visit as the mother-in-law. Rapu had enjoyed showing her around the house and watching as she gasped at all the wealth that now belonged to her daughter.

'Is this heaven or earth?' her mother asked as she ran her hands down the fridge. '*Hei! Chukwu alu go lu m ooooo!* But is it not unhygienic,' she asked, 'to have a toilet inside the house?'

'No,' Rapu said, swallowing the doubts she had always had about the sanitary correctness of doing your business and cooking and eating in the same building. 'Technology takes all the dirt away.'

'What is tekinolodji? Now you start sounding like your brothers.'

Rapu was not entirely sure but it was what Anwuli had told her when she, as green as her mother was now, had asked the same question. Prince, her son, stirring in her arms, gave her an excuse to move her mother's attention to a less murky terrain. There was no need for her to find out just how little she knew.

That was how the first month had been spent: her mother discovering more wonders and Rapu explaining as best she could and Prince keeping them both on their feet. Rapu had no idea that new babies needed so much done for them. She was glad that her mother was there to help her as Mike was of no help at all. Not that she had expected him to be. If truth be told, that first month, she hardly saw anything of him. He bought presents for his son, clothes and toys – so many toys that Rapu had no idea where to store them all – but he spent his nights away and his days in the shop. He was like a man in mourning. Several times upon his return, Rapu caught him walking morosely around the house, touching things that had belonged to Ezi: the round-bottomed mug she had drunk tea out of every morning; the single doily that Ezi had forgotten to take with her when she packed up all the other doilies in the house; her pair of yellow slippers. The few times he smiled, it was at Prince. He would shout for Rapu to bring him the baby. He would hold him for a few minutes in his hands, smiling down at him, before asking Rapu to take him back. Even the bride price, he had paid almost in secret. There was no party to celebrate the new wife. Nothing.

Rapu stayed with her son in her old bedroom, hoping that Mike would invite her into his bed. She belonged there now. She belonged with him. Anwuli told her to be patient. Hot water will eventually cool down. It will not be like this for ever. And I heard from my madam that your madam won't be returning at all.'

'My *madam*?'

'Ah, sorry, oo, your co-wife!'

And that had made both of them laugh, like in the old days, slapping their thighs and giggling until Prince woke and, with a cry louder than their laughter, demanded his mother.

Rapu guarded her home with a ferociousness that her husband had not suspected her to possess. When she eventually got a maid, she would not let her cook or serve Mike's food. She insisted on doing that herself. And one day, after filling himself on her food, and lying alone in his bed, he had suddenly got up and gone to get Rapu.

'Leave the baby,' he said, 'and come and sleep in my bed.'

She had hoped then that she would not be sent back to the guest room. She would have liked to install herself – her Vaseline body lotion, her mentholated powder and a deodorant spray – in the drawers Ezi had cleared out. She was glad to find at the back of one drawer, forgotten, a bottle of perfume which was nearly full and she began to douse herself in it, feeling as if she was becoming Ezi, completely replacing her, not just a callow usurper of her former mistress. She dreamt of a time when her clothes would fill up the cupboards too. Of a time when Mike would no longer yell 'Ezi' when he meant to call her name, when it was she he held tight, swelling inside of her. How humiliated she had felt then, but she had not shown it. She had not told him, 'Hey, I'm not Ezi, ooo, I'm Rapu.'

She knew that patience had its virtues. Like Anwuli said all the time, *Mmili di oku ga emesia juo oyi.* Hot water will always eventually cool down. And she was willing to wait for it to cool. She missed Anwuli. Anwuli who had finally stopped coming to visit her, probably embarrassed by the difference in their stations. And she had not gone to seek her out, grateful to have been spared the burden of making that decision. Once she became a wife in deed to Mike, she found it difficult to pretend that they were on the same level. When Anwuli came over to talk about how much she had saved and what she was going to buy with it, Rapu could not share her enthusiasm. She got a regular allowance from her husband. She no longer needed to scrimp and save for second-hand bargains from the market. And once she had her own house girl, it became even more difficult to keep seeing Anwuli, so when she suddenly stopped visiting, yes, she was grateful. That friendship had served its purpose and had died a natural death.

In the end, Anwuli had married a driver and moved out. When she heard of the upcoming marriage from Anwuli's former mistress, Rapu had bought a set of teacups with matching saucers decorated with pink flowers and blue birds. She had given the present, all wrapped up in shiny wrapping paper, to Anwuli's mistress to give to her old friend. She could not have told Mike she wanted to go to the wedding. He did not even know who Anwuli was. Maids were usually not seen.

Rapu had no idea where Anwuli was; she had not thought about her for years. Until now. With all this talk about Ezi's daughter coming back, she needed a good friend to talk to. As far as she was concerned, this daughter was coming to reap where she did not sow. Ezi was dead and forgotten. Mike never mentioned her. The friends that had once asked about her no longer did, and some of the wives had come to see her as the new mistress, even if they were not friendly. She and Mike had expanded their family. Everything was in order. Then out of the blue, a messenger from home with the news about Mma.

She had dared to ask, 'Why is she coming?' and Mike had responded quickly, 'What do you mean "why"? She's my daughter!'

The tone of his voice carried a warning; there was indignation simmering under it and she did not want it to boil over. She was adept at reading Mike's moods. That was how she had avoided quarrels over the years.

'I only meant why now? Why not before? Not why is she coming? Of course she is your daughter.' She made sure to keep her voice flat, free of any emotion.

'Search me. But it's good.'

'Yes,' Rapu said. 'Indeed it is.' And added to herself, *She's coming into my home. And I'll protect my home with all I've got.* She had not got this far to have Mike give away half of what rightly belonged to her children to a child whose mother abandoned the home many years ago. It was not right. Nobody pushed Ezi out. She got up and walked out. She, Rapu, had put in too much to back down now. Besides, where would she go? She did not have Ezi's advantages. She would not survive alone.

She had never told her children about Mma. Prince took the news in his stride. 'So I have a sister? OK.' But the twins had been very enthusiastic, so enthusiastic, as if the girl coming was coming especially for them. Rapu had scolded them.

When the day of Mma's visit finally arrived, Rapu was determined to make her so uncomfortable that she would leave. But she had to be subtle, so that Mike was not pushed to fight for his daughter. Men were like that. Push them and you push them away. She would not repeat Ezi's mistakes. She, Rapu, was smarter. Her mother had taught her well.

Even in the first months when Mike called her 'Ezi', Rapu never feared that he would go after his wife. What she feared most was that Ezi would realise what a huge mistake she had made and come back and take over, relegating her to her old room again. If she ever went back there, there was no hope of her climbing up again. And she had to be up. She had to stay up, not just for her sake but for her parents and her children. Her father said that the gods had fulfilled their promise beyond his expectations: 'Ah, if only there is a way I can repay Ajofia. Oh, but I am sure Ajofia is being feted by our ancestors, he could not fail to be for bringing our family so much good news.'

The first time he came to Kaduna, to his daughter's house, his eyes shone with a new admiration for his little girl. It did not matter now what his sons did, how long they decided to go to school for – his daughter had wiped the spittle off his face. Mike took him to see a doctor for his backache, he got a full check-up and was saddled with drugs. He came home repeating, '*Ogbenye ajoka*. Poverty is bad. All the illness I had, the aches and pain I had, everything gone. I thought it was old age, but now I know it was just poverty.'

The only thing he refused to do was to have his blood taken. 'I haven't got much blood in me, I'm not about to give away the little I have. And what sort of witchery is this? Only witches want blood.' The doctor had let him go without the test.

Rapu was used to being a madam now, used to thinking that everything belonged to her family. No way would she allow that to change.

Part 3

Si kele onye nti chiri; enu anughi, ala anu.

Salute the deaf; if the heavens don't hear, the earth
will hear.

Igbo proverb

Kaduna, January 2002

1

'Come in,' Rapu said, her smile almost too wide for her face as she moved aside to let Mma enter. Mma's first thought was that Madam Gold was wrong. Rapu was not skinny at all. There was no chewing stick-like quality to her. Her arms were copious. The woman was almost as big as Madam Gold. There was nothing to link this woman before her to the Rapu she had imagined.

Mma walked in and a man came forward to hug her before she had a chance to look at him properly. She would have liked to drink him in, to extend this moment before her dreams blurred into reality.

F is for father. Father smelt strongly of aftershave. His hug was tight, as if he never wanted to let go. He was much taller than she was. Now she knew who she got her height from.

'My daughter, welcome,' he said and led her to sit beside him.

'Today I am a very happy man. You've come back to me.'

He did not look too different from the old photograph of him she had found. Where there had been an afro in the photograph, there was now a bald patch, shiny with sweat. She felt like reaching out and wiping his head.

229

F is for father. Father has a bald patch. Father lives in a big house in Kaduna. My father. Mine!

Madam Gold had told her how to behave. To apologise to her father on her mother's behalf. To offer a gift. Mma reached into her bag and pulled out the two bottles of gin. 'For you, Papa,' she said. The word had come naturally. Her mother had been Mum. Mummy sometimes. But her father could not be Dad. Not Daddy. Those words had an intimacy that she could not claim at this moment. Papa suggested a comfort, a hope for something more. It was too early to call him anything else. He looked relieved and smiled as he accepted the bottles. Then he said, 'You should meet the rest of your family.'

The names and faces passed her by in a blur. Prince. Then the sixteen-year-old twins, Chioma and Chindu. 'My daughters,' her father said, as the girls whispered shy hellos, their faces lit up by the same identical smile. They looked very much like their father. And, Mma thought with a sense of pride, that meant they looked like her. They had the same rich dark complexion of polished mahogany. And lips that turned slightly upwards. It would be obvious to anyone that they were related. 'My daughters' Mma heard over and over again in her head. 'My daughters.' Not, 'Your sisters.' The way her father had claimed them so casually. Would he claim her that way too? 'This is Mma, my daughter!'

Food was brought out by Rapu and a maid, a small sturdy girl with plaited hair that stood like nails on her head. They came out carrying platters: steaming bowls of pounded yam and soup. Once the aroma of the egusi wafted up to her, tears stung Mma's eyes. Her mother's last meal.

'Let us go and eat.' Her father shepherded them to the huge table in one corner of the room. 'Sit.' Mma sat. Her father sat to the right of her, at the head of the table. Rapu sat opposite her. Prince sat on the other side of Mma and his sisters sat beside their mother. They took their places without arguing, as if they sat there every day. Or perhaps, they had been told beforehand where to sit. How to act.

'When I heard of your mother's death, I was very sorry,' her father said. He sounded formal. Not at all like he sounded when he asked Prince to get a bottle of water from the fridge or one of the girls to get him his pill from the table. He did not have to explain which pill. Or which table. She knew which one. That was how families worked.

J is for jealousy. J. Jay. She heard of the jay first from her mother. A jay is a colourful bird. The first time she heard the word jailbird, she had misheard it as jay bird. Her mother had explained the difference. She imagined her mother in this house, living with a co-wife and her children. No matter how hard she tried, she could not do it. She could see her mother on Neni Street, sharing her life with no one. Her mother would never have been able to dance here. It would have been impossible. She could feel it. This house would not have accepted her mother's twirling in her red dancing shoes, laughing her loud laugh.

She dunked a ball of pounded yam into the soup. How often had she thought of it? Just a pinch of otapiapia in her mother's food and she would be rid of her. She

231

knew she could never do it but it did not stop her from thinking it. How often had she dreamt of this? Of being with her father. But she had always thought of him in a vacuum, as if he were somewhere waiting for her to come to continue his life. But his life had never stopped. On the walls were photographs of his family. His son and daughters. There were none of her. It was as though she did not exist for him, as though she did not belong here. There were no photographs of her mother either. Whatever life Ezi had lived here had been erased. Mma tried to eat but the lump in her throat refused to dislodge and so she asked, quite without meaning to, 'Why did you hide from me?'

Her father, to the right of her, held his lump in mid-air. Rapu looked up from her food, a grin on her face, as if the question had been asked especially for her entertainment.

'I've never hidden from you,' he said at last. 'Why would I hide? I never moved.'

He told Mma of the year 2000, when riots flared up over the introduction of sharia law, and his supermarket, long seen as a symbol of Igbo success in Hausaland, was burnt down. He had refused to join the throng of Igbos hastily boarding buses at the Mandia motor park heading back to Onitsha and Owerri and Enugu, shouting slogans such as, 'Give us Biafra back! Nigeria has disappointed us! No more one Nigeria!' Kaduna was his home and there was no way he could think of it, or of himself in it, as alien. He had never managed to feel at home anywhere but in the north. When Rapu begged him, afraid for their children's lives, he still refused. His house was not in Sabon Gari where southerners were dragged out and massacred. One of the wisest decisions he had taken was to build a house in the middle of a Hausa neighbourhood. Nobody would dare descend on an area as exclusive as this, and his Hausa neighbours would never shop him to a head-hunting mob. He had never left.

'Did your mother tell you I was hiding?' He sounded slightly amused.

'No,' she said, wishing she had never spoken. There was an uneasy silence descending on the table. She could tell, without looking, that everybody had stopped eating. They were waiting for . . . what?

'You could always have found me.'

'But I didn't even know about you!' She had to fight to keep from shouting. This was not the welcome she had envisaged. And this house, this strange house with its hard leather cushions and a high ceiling and a chandelier, was not home. Home had a colour TV with a remote control that no longer worked; home had a balcony which looked out to the hills rising above the city; it had a bedroom with her mother's pictures on the wall. Home smelt differently. She was tired. She wanted to lie down and sleep. She would wake up in better spirits. She was sure of that.

'Listen, this is neither the time nor the place to apportion blame. But if you never heard of me, it is your mother's fault. But that does not matter now, does it? You've come back where you belong. You've come home. That's all that matters. You've come back to make amends.'

S is for sins. What is a sin? At Catechism, she was taught to repeat, 'Sin is an offence against reason, truth and right conscience.' But she could not tell what sins she was supposed to be atoning for. What were her mother's sins? Mma swallowed all the words she wanted to say and started eating the food she no longer tasted. She answered questions quietly and briefly. It was the way she used to respond to her mother. 'Yes.' 'No.' 'Now leave me to finish my novel.' But she was careful to be polite with her father. She was always polite with strangers. She caught Rapu's eye, who smiled at her. 'Some more food?' Rapu asked.

'No, thank you.' The woman could see that her plate was still full. There was something about her that Mma, in the first five minutes of meeting her, did not like. Her sweetness seemed put on. S is for saccharine, she thought, as she rolled another ball of pounded yam, ready to be dipped in the soup. S is for a sugar-coated smile, for a sugar-coated question which meant nothing at all. Too much sweet is cloying. That smile, too wide, too sweet, was starting to hurt Mma. She did not want to see it again.

She smiled back at Rapu. A tired, worn smile. Ezi never smiled unless she meant it. Mma learnt to smile even when she would rather not. Now she turned her eyes on her father. It was funny, she thought, how first her grandfather and now her father had assumed she had sought them out to make reparations. Why should she be apologising for a woman who was not sorry for what she did? And a woman who, she now realised, had done nothing wrong? She was developing a respect for her mother; she would never apologise for her. But Madam Gold had told her, 'Do not be stubborn. It's the way things are done here. You do not have to say Sorry, *ndo*. Your actions say it for you, so let them. Do not dispute in words what your gestures tell your family. It makes no sense. In Igboland, we say a lot more by what we do than by what we voice out. So give your father the bottles of gin. He'll understand. And your mother, I am sure, will understand that you had to do this. She was stubborn but she would have wanted you to be happy.'

Mma felt treacherous but she believed Madam Gold. If she had any hope of being accepted, of living a normal life with Obi, she had to do this. She had to pretend. Lie-lie too much and it becomes the truth.

'Any young man eyeing you?' Roll. Dip. Swallow.

'Yes, sir. We hope to get married soon.' Roll. Dip. Swallow.

'Good. He has to come and meet me. Pay your bride price like I paid your mother's. Don't worry, I won't ask him for much. I've got enough to last my children and I. But he has to obey the rules of tradition.' Roll. Dip. Swallow.

'Yes, sir.' S is for sins. She had to make reparations for that. S is for stranger. S is for sir. It's what you called your father if you'd never lived with him. If you did not know where his medication box was. If you did not even know what he was taking medication for. No, sir. Yes, sir. S is for strangers multiplied by five. Ten eyes watching her, sizing her up, maybe wondering what she was doing there. What was she doing here? And all this talk of tradition, which had pushed her mother away in the first place. Roll. Dip. Swallow. She had met her father. She had met Rapu. She had met her brother and sisters. After all the build-up to this day, there was

235

something disappointing in how she felt. Whatever it was she had expected to feel on this day, it had fallen short of her hopes. For the first time, she missed her mother. Yes, Mummy. No, Mummy. Even when she hated her, she was still Mummy. Mummy was a name and nothing more, but it still suggested a certain degree of intimacy.

For much of her adult life, she had felt nothing for her mother. There was no intimacy, no warm love. She did not go to her with problems. She did not talk to her about the young men who loved her and then dumped her. She did not, like her friend Adaku, beg to wear her shoes, her dresses, as if they were not mother and daughter but sisters. Nor was she like Constance, who was her mother's tongue; she could, like an attentive lover, finish off her mother's sentences, so that people admired their closeness and said that in a previous life they must have been twins who could not bear to be parted and had reincarnated as mother and daughter.

No. Mma and her mother were simply two shadows living together, the older one taking care of the younger: providing the three necessities of shelter, food and clothing. They took turns cooking. It was Mma who had insisted on drawing up a rota. The kitchen was too small for two, she said, when her mother said they should cook together. And her mother had not argued – 'Whatever suits you' – as if she had spent her entire life giving in to her daughter's whims and desires. The thought of being cooped up in there with her mother, their elbows touching while one chopped onions and the other washed pepper, was something Mma could not bear.

They ate separately, Mma in her bedroom with its walls papered with posters of famous models, wondering what their lives must be like, and her mother mostly in the sitting room, watching Bollywood films with impossible names and casts of flighty women with dark shiny hair. 'Did you know,' her mother asked her once, 'that Indian women keep their hair glossy with coconut oil?'

'No,' she had answered flatly, not even feigning interest. 'And I do not care,' she'd added to discourage any further talk. That was how their relationship was. Aborted conversations about nothing that really mattered, at least not to Mma.

If her mother had ever spoken to her about her father, if she had once said, 'Did you know, Mma, that your father and I met . . .' Mma would have dropped whatever she was doing and would have given her mother her full and undivided attention. But no.

She was here now with her father. Roll. Dip. Swallow. It was difficult swallowing. Painful. As if she had a fish bone stuck in her throat.

It would do no good to start crying here, but the upside-down thoughts she had of her mother came back to her. Right there, eating egusi. They wanted to drown her. She had killed her mother. Her ears were clogged and her father had to ask several times before she heard.

'Why are you not eating?'

'I'm full, sir.'

'Already? Ah ah?'

'She has just met her father. No wonder she has no appetite.' Rapu looked at her, her wide smile still there. Its too-much-sweetness turned Mma's stomach.

'You young people of nowadays. I hope my daughter

237

is not starving herself so she can look like all those skinny things on TV?'

'No, sir. Thank you, sir. Thank you.' She turned to Rapu. The smell of egusi was becoming too much. She turned to her brother. 'So what do you do, Prince?' She had to speak to keep the thoughts away. Her face felt taut, pulled like the skin over a drum, and she feared it would burst if she did not distract herself.

Rapu answered, grinning from ear to ear. 'Prince is a doctor, he's doing his internship.' A smile lit up her eyes.

'My son, the doctor,' her father said, and the pride in his voice hit Mma with the sharpness of a blade. S is for son. Son. It needs no explanation. The pride in the voice. How would he introduce Mma? My daughter? My daughter by my first wife? You remember her? Ezi? The one who upped and left with the baby and never looked back and now she's dead and her daughter has come to ask me to forgive her. And I've forgiven her. I've welcomed my daughter. My daughter, Mma. Would the pride be in his voice? Would it be sweet and warm like it was when he talked about his other children?

'Yes, just graduated,' Prince said. 'Still thinking of specialisation. Not sure what branch I want to settle in.'

'I've told him to go in for neurosurgery, that's where the money is,' Mike said.

'Which ones are you thinking of?' Mma asked

'It's a toss-up between nephrology and gynaecology. They've got nothing to do with each other, but they both fascinate me. I'm not really into neurosurgery, though Daddy is.'

Daddy. Spoken with such ease. Mma felt out of place.

238

She murmured something inaudible to Prince and did not say another word. Mike finished his plate of food, washed his hands and ordered Mma to go and rest. 'Rapu will show you to your room,' her father said. 'You must be tired. It's been a long day.'

She would be shown to her room. Like a guest. What else could she be? She was alarmed at the thoughts forming and growing in her head, at the discontent she was already feeling, at the frustration she could not pinpoint the reason for. Nobody had sent her on this quest. She had initiated it. It was her lifelong dream, so why was she feeling so terrible?

The room was an all-pink affair, probably painted for the twins when they were born and never redecorated. The paint was flaking in places. Like old skin failing to rejuvenate. She wondered, not for the first time, how it must have felt to have grown up here. There was no radio, and the house was quiet. This was the sort of silence Mma had imagined she wanted when her mother lived. S is for silence. Silence in which to think. In which to re-imagine her life, to revise her history. There are different kinds of silences. And the silence covering this house was the kind in which her guilt shouted in her ears. She lay in bed crying, begging for her mother's forgiveness for what she had done. She was changing in ways she could never have imagined.

That first night, her mother appeared to her in a dream. This time she did not stand at the door of Mma's room in Enugu but at the door of the bedroom Mma was in, in her father's house. Her eyes glistened like diamonds and tears streaked down her cheeks in sparkly trails. Mma knew that her mother was crying for her, expiating her for her sins. She felt a closeness to her mother in that instant, as if they had been melded together, and she felt her mother's breath at the nape of her neck and her hands squeezing hers, and when she woke up, there was a lightness in her head and a soft song humming in her ears lulling her back to sleep again.

She had wanted her mother dead. She had willed it. She had thought several times of what it would be like to mix otapiapia in her mother's food. The day her mother complained of cramps worrying-worrying her for the first time, Mma was sure she was to blame. How else to explain the cramps that started after Ezi ate the fufu and soup that she had made? What if she had, as she had stood there thinking her upside-down thoughts, let some poison drop? What if she had actually scooped a thumbful of the otapiapia and mixed it but had forgotten about it? One read about this all the time. People who did things so terrible that the only way they could deal with their action was to repress the memory of it. What if she had repressed the memory? If an upside-down thought ate at you every day, gnawed at you like determined mice gnawing at food, never letting up, what were the chances that you would not be helpless to resist it? But after last night's dream, the smell that had dogged her nose cleared, and she could breathe easy again. She got out of bed, whispered thanks to her mother and for the first time in many years began to hum a song. Then she began to sing.

Obu onye ga-di ka nne m
Nne m oo
O bu onye ga-adi ka nne m
Nne m o.

She sang that song to celebrate her mother, celebrating all mothers, all good mothers who daily, silently, perform acts of sacrifice, immolate themselves in little daily rituals to save their children.

2

On the roads of Kaduna rumours were swirling like a hurricane, making their way to the breakfast table. The maid had heard, when she went to buy bread, that riots were breaking out downtown because of a newspaper article. Mike dispelled the words with a wave of his hand. How very like her mother, Mma thought, and wondered who had picked up the gesture from whom. Ezi had always been able to dismiss arguments, no matter how tight the logic or heated the debate, with a swift wave of her hand. That was enough to say, *I am done with this*. And then she would laugh that loud, high laugh of hers. But Mike did not laugh. Instead he spoke. 'Kaduna has learnt its lesson,' he said. 'There is no way the city will tolerate another riot. Kaduna has learnt the hard way that it has to accommodate all its peoples. And if anything were to happen, we are safe, the same as last time. It is the southerners in Sabon Gari who need to fear.' He had always been against segregation. 'You move to a place,' he said, 'you move into its heart! All this creating your own neighbourhood only causes problems. We live happily among the Hausa and no one will dare to come anywhere near here. There's no need to worry, it is all a lot of talk. Nobody is going to go to war over a journalist's claim that the Prophet Muhammad, had he been alive, would have chosen a wife among the beauty contestants.'

'You have too much faith in this town,' Rapu said, passing him a glass of water. Hissing under her breath, 'You have too much faith in people', in such a way that made Mma wonder if there was something else behind her words. When Mma caught her eyes, she looked balefully over her head to a spot on the wall. Prince and the two girls, identical in their matching dresses, smiled shyly at Mma, the same way they had when they had been introduced to her the day before.

'This city does not reward faith,' Rapu said, reaching across the table to set the carafe with water down in the middle. She never raised her voice as she spoke.

'This is my home,' Mike said, ending the conversation. 'I wouldn't give Kaduna up for anything. Did you sleep well, Mma?'

'Yes, sir.'

The rest of the meal was eaten in silence, then everyone dispersed to their rooms. Mike said he had to run into town to 'do one or two things'. By the time he came back, it was time for lunch.

Mma had hoped to be able to talk to her father alone, to have some time with him, just the two of them. It was not as if she had any secrets to tell him, but she had imagined that after years of not seeing her, he would be curious about her, hungry for some time alone, the way her grandfather had been. She did not want to share him with three other children he had known all their lives, feeding him titbits of her life through mouthfuls of food. 'Are you enjoying your meal? Did you sleep well? Was your bed comfortable? Was the air conditioner

243

in your room cool enough? Is there a man in your life?'
She wanted him to ask her about things that mattered,
to show that all through the years she had wondered
about him, without even having an idea of what he
looked like, he had thought of her, too.

Rapu asked Prince to pass her the carton of juice
beside him. She poured out a glass for herself and then
asked Mma, 'So, do you work?' Her smile was the same
wide, wide smile. Sugar-coated, Mma thought. Saccharine
smile.

'Yes,' Mma said before she could stop herself. 'I work
in a bank.' This was no time to reveal that she was living
off her mother's wealth. Granted, it was not a good way
to start off the relationship with her just-discovered
family, but the question caught her unawares and the
tone in which it was asked was suspicious. Maybe she
was imagining too much. But with her doctor brother
and the twins doing brilliantly at school, she did not
want to appear unambitious.

She was not a scrounger and she would put her
mother's money to good use. She would invest the capital
and prove that she was her mother's daughter. Better to
let them think she was a young professional woman.
She would tell her father the truth. But not just yet.
When the time was right, when he knew her well
enough to realise that she was bright and capable. Her
father smiled approvingly at her bank-job declaration.

'It's always a good place to start from. Banks,' he said.
'So what did you actually study? Economics? Finance?
Accounting?'

'No. Theatre arts.' Mma dreaded this question. People
always assumed that she had studied theatre arts because

she lacked the brains and the aptitude for a more demanding course but the fact was that she could have done whatever course she had wanted to. They did not see her passion for theatre, they had never seen her on stage.

'Oh,' her father said. She could see he was disappointed.

'Ah,' Rapu said and smiled her smile. 'The banks take all degrees these days.'

Mma said nothing in response. Nobody spoke and for a long while they ate in silence. Mike began to speak of the weather, complaining of the dryness of Kaduna in November, of how hard it had been to get his super-market back on its feet after losing everything, and how he had resorted to selling exotic blinds. He never mentioned Ezi. All the while, Rapu kept up a smile whenever Mma caught her eyes. Mma wanted that smile wiped off. She wished her father would mention her mother, talk about the love that had brought them together. This woman had the waist of a wrestler, but a face that did not look much older than Mma's and a smile that curled like a snake. Mma could not stand it.

Mma was relieved that she was leaving the next day. Her mission was accomplished: she had met the family, had met her siblings. But as for getting close to her father, she would take it at his pace. She would let him lead. Now she was here she could see that there was no hurry at all. That she had wasted years hating her mother for no reason. In her own way, her mother had tried to make her strong. She could see that now. And she was grateful.

Chioma and Chindu continued to discuss in quiet tones the Miss World contest, their voices sounding so alike that they could be interchanged, hardly rising above the noise of the table except when they asked their father a question. It was only their eyes, shiny and huge, that revealed the extent of their excitement. Mma felt a temporary stab of jealousy, so sharp that she let out an 'ouch', as if she had been pricked by a pin. Luckily for her, no one seemed to have noticed. The girls kept on talking. How exciting it was, wasn't it, that Kaduna was hosting the Miss World competition? And in their lifetime. What an opportunity! How lovely it would be if they could go, if they could catch a glimpse of the contestants, be near such glamour. And Agbani would be there! Agbani, their model idol. They yearned to be like her. Beautiful. Ah, Agbani's face is so smooth. Who would have thought that a Nigerian would be Miss World? They could be too. Didn't that girl come up to them one day and ask them if they were related to Agbani? It would be nice to go and see the contestants in the flesh. See Agbani. They knew a girl whose father was someone important and who had got a ticket to go and watch, with the promise to be taken backstage to meet the eventual winner. How much luckier could one person get? Daddy, don't you know anyone who could get us a ticket?

'It probably won't go ahead,' Prince said, working through a plate of rice. 'Not with all the wahala over it now.' He had a deep voice. A voice sure of its place and its power. Mma could imagine showing him off.

'But the organisers are determined to let it happen,' Mma said, dropping her spoon and spitting rice as she

246

spoke. 'I don't think a few dissenting voices will make them back down now. You saw the news yesterday.' She wiped her mouth with the back of her hand, streaking it with oil.

'A few dissenting voices, eh?' Rapu asked, sounding angrier than the occasion required. It was the first time Mma heard her voice rise. 'These are not a few dissenting voices. Theirs is the voice of the majority. *Oranaeze*. You should walk down the street and hear the amount of outrage that there is. And the article the paper ran today will only make things worse.'

'You are such a pessimist, Rapu,' Mike said. 'I saw the article. I don't think it will lead to trouble just because a few hoodlums say it will. I mean, when I was out this morning, there was only a handful of touts hanging around.'

'And you, Mike, always see the best in people,' Rapu said in the flattest voice, as if she was discussing what sort of fish to make for dinner.

Mma was sure there was more behind Rapu's words than mere disagreement over the seriousness of the article. The suspicion had been building up that Rapu resented her, and so she dissected her every word, looking for proof. What she would do with the evidence, she did not know.

'We were better off with the military in charge. They knew how to deal with people who took the law into their own hands,' Rapu continued. 'We would not have this mayhem now. The country started falling apart once they left.'

'But, Mama, are you saying that a dictatorship is better for us?' Prince asked. 'Nobody should prefer a military dictatorship to a democracy, no matter how flawed the democracy is!' He had switched to English, as if he could make his points more persuasive by articulating them in another language. 'And besides, I see no mayhem.'

'See you talking like you've swallowed a dictionary, like your uncles,' Rapu replied in Igbo. 'Some good all that education did them. And what good is all that grammar if the country is on its head? How long was it after the military left that the clashes erupted like rashes? In Shagamu it was the Yoruba killing Hausa; in Lagos and Onitsha, human beings are set on fire for stealing, even when there is no proof of theft. Imagine Idiagbon in power. He would have put a stop to all this nonsense. *Odogwu!*'

Mma felt out of place. She turned to one of the twins and asked what they had planned for that evening. She would like to leave the house, see something beyond the front yard she had walked around several times already.

'We're going to visit our friend.'

'Oh,' Mma said, disappointed. 'I had hoped you could take me round Kaduna. You know, show me a bit of the city. I brought my camera and I haven't even taken a single photograph!'

'Ah, not today, oo,' Rapu intervened. 'Tension is too high. Too much. This is not the right time to be walking around Kaduna taking pictures. Nobody leaves the house today, *biko*. You all stay inside; let me know where my ailment stems from, *ka m malu nke m na-aya biko*. Papa, Prince, tell them please.'

'But I'm leaving tomorrow,' Mma said, looking at her father as if begging for his support. 'You said yourself that things could not be that bad.'

248

'But you'll come back again. All I'm saying is that the streets are not safe for young girls to go walking about. This is your father's house and I am sure we haven't seen the last of you,' Rapu said, before Mike could answer.

Mma was certain now that there was an animosity in Rapu's voice when she spoke about this being her father's house, thinly veiled but possible to make out. What was the problem with this woman? She would not dwell on it, as no one else seemed to have noticed. Instead, she bent her head over her plate, chewing her food contemplatively as if it contained all the answers she would ever need.

She did not want her memory of the visit to be spoilt by Rapu. Or for the lightness she felt on waking up to be weighed down by her animosity. Almost as if we were co-wives, she thought.

'Of course she will come back,' Mike said, grinning. 'This is your home too. When next you come back, your sisters will take you around and show off their big sister. But for today, I think you should stay indoors, until we are sure what the real situation is at least.'

It had been agreed that Mike would take her to the airport the next day. He was so much the opposite of her mother, who could talk for hours. She had not even had a chance yet to tell him properly about Obi. About their plans to move to Kaduna. She could afford any house here. She had not told him yet that she would like to get married in Kaduna, to have him walk her down the aisle, to show off her family to Obi's parents. This was the sort of family anybody would be proud to belong to. Old money. Earned through hard work. A brother who was going to specialise in something impressive. And twin sisters beautiful in their identical way. She would tell him in the car, away from the ubiquitous presence of Rapu.

Maybe her sisters would be her bridesmaids. Her thoughts skipped away into a future that conveniently ignored Rapu. After the long lunch of rice and chicken, one of her sisters asked her if she wanted to play a game, to compensate for not being able to go out. Mike shouted, 'Wonderful', clapping his hands like an excited school boy. 'What a wonderful idea. Bring out the WHOT and we will all play together. Your mother, Mma, was like you. Anywhere she went, she wanted to go out and see the city. But I hope you like to play too? She did not like to sit still and play. There was this time we went to the Game Reserve in Bauchi. Your mother insisted on taking walks every day. I just wanted to lie down in bed and rest. I had only agreed to go to escape the noise of the city. She had wanted to go because she wanted to see all those animals and take long walks!' His eyes shone.

It was the first time he had spoken about Ezi to Mma. She had not known that her mother was a nature lover, the way she refused to let her keep any pets. Or maybe she thought it was imprisoning them. How was Mma to have known? Ezi had not been one to explain herself to people, least of all to her daughter. She had always annoyingly responded to Mma's numerous Whys with the childish, 'Because Y has a long tail and two branches.' Or with the equally annoying, 'Curiosity killed the cat.' When Mma learnt to counter with, 'But satisfaction brought it back to life', her mother would add, 'Cats

250

cannot be resurrected', and that, for her, was the end of the conversation.

The cards were shuffled and Mike slapped hard on the table. He then placed a fourteen on top of it. 'Go to market, all of you!' As they picked cards from the pile, Mma felt that her life was complete. This was the picture she had always carried in her head of the sort of family she wanted to belong to. And now she did. She held her cards over her face to shield them from the others and she let out a wide smile.

3

She set the alarm on her mobile phone for 7 a.m. and settled into her bed. It had been a lovely evening. After the card game they had had a much more relaxed supper. Mma felt new anger at her mother for having denied it to her. They could all have got on well. But this thought – of how her mother and not Rapu would have been the mistress of the house; of how theirs would not have been the first polygamous home; of how Ezi should have tried to work things through; of how selfish her mother had been to give it all up – all these thoughts, which would have come swiftly and made her surly in the past, now came haltingly, as if she had lost her sure-footedness, as if she were no longer certain of her place in the world. The same way she was not sure of her place in her father's world. She was grateful to have found Mike, she just did not know if there was a place for her in this house.

She could not imagine moving around here with the same ease that she did back in Enugu. She had taken her shower quietly, unwilling to disturb the silence. Moving to Kaduna, being close to him but not living with him, would give them both a chance to build a relationship. They could grow on each other. Prince, while not unfriendly, was aloof, but she would enjoy having her sisters in the neighbourhood. She could take them shopping, buy them things they did not need – that was a big sister's prerogative. They were still too young for make-up but she imagined them coming to her for tips in a few years. There were times in her earlier life where she had wished for a sibling to complain to about their mother. If she moved to Kaduna, her sisters would have her to complain to about their parents. She remembered being their age. It was the age when parents got it all wrong.

The alarm did not go off. A frantic knocking on her door woke Mma up. At first she thought it was the radio but it was one of the twins – she found it difficult to tell them apart – who got her out of bed, asking had she heard the news? Kaduna was up in flames. Mma thought how very melodramatic of her to use that term, as if the city were on fire. 'What is happening?' she asked.

'Kaduna is burning,' the girl replied, eyes blazing as if mirroring the fire. Mma put on a robe and went into the sitting room where everyone was gathered in front of the TV, listening to the state governor remind the citizens that they were all members of one Nigeria.

'There is no Muslim Nigeria and no Christian Nigeria. There is only one indivisible Nigeria. Kaduna belongs to all Nigerians. No religion endorses violence or gratuitous cruelty. Regrettably, some undesirable elements have incited these ugly clashes and those elements will be fished out and properly punished. A curfew has been put in place . . .'

There were clips of houses burning and corpses left

253

out on the streets. There was a close-up of a woman's scarf.

'There are clashes downtown between Muslims and Christians,' her father said, as if Mma could have missed it, taking his eyes off the TV for a minute. The newspaper article had indeed sparked protests, just as Rapu had predicted.

The offices of the paper that carried the article had been targeted and set on fire. According to the news, some Christians in the neighbourhood saw that as an open call to war and now there were sporadic fights erupting all over town. 'You can't leave today, oo, Mma,' one of the twins announced.

Mike groaned and Mma knew that he was worrying about his business. It was easy to see from the name it proudly displayed on its front that it was owned by a Southern Christian. If there were people intent on destroying Christian property to avenge the slight on their religion, they would not spare it. He did not dare drive that far to check on it, and not having any news of it made him anxious and short-tempered.

'We'll be lucky to be spared this time. We should have left here after the sharia riots,' Rapu said. And then in the silence that followed, she added, 'And now with your daughter springing herself on us!' She turned to Mma. 'If you were hoping for a slice of your father's wealth, you can think again. See what a precarious position our business is in now.'

Mma felt the words as she would a slap across her face. So that was what it was all about. The eyes following her around. The snide remarks delivered in that flat voice, saccharine smile. Rapu believed that she had sought out

254

her father for money. She wanted to laugh, to tell this woman that the money her mother left her could buy her this house ten times over. She had more money than she could ever finish in this lifetime.

'Rapu, stop,' her father said, his voice lacking authority or conviction, but strong enough to send Rapu sulking into the kitchen.

Mma went back to her room and did not come out again. She knew that her father had other things on his mind, but he could have supported her. Her mother would have. She felt a sudden pang again. When she refused to come out for lunch, one of the twins came with a tray of food for her. 'Please, join us for dinner tonight,' she said. Mma was touched, and promised she would.

By evening, it was obvious that the situation was far worse than anyone had imagined. A fatwa had been placed on the offending journalist's head and the deputy governor of a neighbouring state had come on air to announce that: 'It is binding on all Muslims, wherever they are, to consider the killing of the writer as a religious duty.'

Everybody was back in the sitting room, plates of food on their laps, their eyes glued to the TV, which was churning out news by the minute.

'How irresponsible of him,' Prince shouted, as if the deputy governor were right there in the sitting room with them. 'How can he say that? He has a responsibility to make sure this doesn't escalate. How do such idiots get elected?'

'But she shouldn't have written that,' Rapu said. 'That was irresponsible too. What did she honestly think would happen? That she would be lauded?'

'We live in a democratic country, Mama. There is freedom of speech. Freedom of press.'

'Freedom this, freedom that. Of what use is that freedom without common sense?'

Prince started to say something, stopped, looked at Mma as if asking her for her support. Mma was more upset that, because of this journalist, she could not leave. She wanted to go home. To Obi. But it was the first time her brother had sought her help. She said, 'We should value freedom above all else. This is a free country, people should be free to write what they want to write.'

'Freedom above common sense? I'm not surprised you'd think that. I still say bring back the military,' Rapu said and then shouted for the maid. 'Mmachi! Mmachi! Get me a glass of water. Quick!'

Prince replicated his mother's cloying smile. He said, 'A dictatorship is bad for the people, it's bad for our image.'

'Where's that girl? In my day, maids were quick on their feet. This one walks like a tortoise.' Rapu gave out a long hiss. 'And you think all this rioting and killing is good for your image? And for your people? Your father's shop – you think democracy will save it? Or this house if our neighbours turn against us?'

The twins sat quietly through it all, mourning a beauty contest that was not to be. Mike kept his eyes on the TV, watching to see if his shop would be shown, razed to nothing.

The next two days were spent like this: Mike muttering and pacing around, wondering if his shop still stood;

Rapu, talking of how their lives were finished, they should have left when they had a chance; and Mma, feeling strangled in a house that was becoming increasingly small with each passing minute, saying very little. She began to feel like a visitor to whom the end of the yam was being served, the bit reserved for unwanted guests.

By the following day, Rapu's insinuations had become more frequent. And Mike no longer asked her to stop. At dinner that night, a sombre dinner with only Mma, her father and Rapu, as nobody else was in the mood to eat at the table, Rapu began again.

'If you've come hoping for some money, your father has none to spare. You've seen our three children.'

Mma could not believe her ears. Rapu's smile across from her was smug. Full. Proprietorial.

She tried not to cry. 'I haven't come for money. I only came because I was curious, curious about my father. Curious about the man who had me and then hid himself from me.'

'I did not hide. I've told you before. A man who wants to hide does not hide in his house. You could have found me. Your mother made her bed. I did not make it for her. She left. As God is my witness, she walked out of here on her own two feet. Did she say I asked her to leave? Did anyone tell you that?'

'But why? Why did she leave?' Mma's voice was rising, the anger palpable, her eyes strokes of lightning as they went from Mike to Rapu and back again. She no longer cared about being rude, about offending the family she had found.

'I did not do anything many other men haven't done

before me. I was patient with your mother. More patient than most. More patient than her father had been with her own mother. Your mother thought she was the Queen of England. She learnt nothing from her family, her friends. Her mother warned her against leaving. Nobody sent her out. She—'

Mma could no longer listen. She broke in, 'So that makes it OK? To sleep with the . . . the—'

'The what?' Rapu challenged. 'Whatever I might have been, this is my home now and you'd do well to remember it, young lady. You think you can come in here and hustle your way into the family? Well, you are no match for me. Even your mother was no match for me, as mad as she was.' Her laughter was crazed.

'Stop it!' Mike shouted, banging a fist on the table. 'Don't you ever talk about Ezi like that again!'

Rapu's laughter died, and rapidly muttering something she got up and blundered through the sitting room, almost toppling her chair in her haste. Mike held his head in his hands and Mma wondered if she should apologise. The food was untouched. She pushed her chair back and began to get up when her father held out a hand to stop her. She sat back down. Her father looked at her, bowed his head as if he was ashamed and then he said, 'She came back. She came back once with you. She said it was to give us another chance. I thought she had changed her mind. For her to have come all the way. I thought . . . I was very happy. I loved her. I loved her so much. She begged me to send Rapu away. But it was impossible. I had married her by then. Ezi wanted her daughter to have a father. I begged her, too. I wanted to be a father to my son. Either I kept the two of you, or I kept my son. What sort of a choice was that?'

Mma felt the room blurring and begin to lose its definition. She heard herself shout, 'She came back? She came back!' She began to cry.

She cried for the mother, for she could see now the woman who was betrayed, who could not stay. She cried for all the times she had wished her mother dead. She cried that her mother had left before she got a chance to know her, to appreciate the sacrifice she went through to raise her. She cried until there were no more tears to be found in her. And what tears she had shed burnt her face.

She felt her father's hands rubbing her shoulders, kneading them as if he were kneading flour for chin-chin. She tried to shake them off. He held on tighter. Even though he was standing behind her, she heard his voice as if he was speaking from a tunnel.

'Your mother . . . I never stopped loving your mother. What Rapu said now about you wanting my money, she shouldn't have. You're entitled to it.'

'I don't want your money! My mother was rich!'

'Your mother was a wonderful woman. When she left, my world ended.'

'But you picked it up just fine!' Mma managed to shake his hands off this time. 'Why did you do it?'

It was a quieter voice that said through the tunnel, 'A moment of weakness. I don't know. I'm not proud of it but I do not regret my children.'

'You betrayed her!'

'And she punished me enough for it.' His voice grew louder. 'She should have stayed.'

'She came back, you said so.'

'She knew I could never do what she wanted me to. No one asks a man to give up his son.' His voice was low, his tone measured.

'You don't know how much she suffered! What I suffered.' Her voice was a wire winding itself around her throat. It sank into a whisper. 'I suffered. I suffered. I suffered.' Trot. Trot. Trot. It cantered into a silence so absolute she could hear her father breathing behind her.

His hands were no longer on her shoulders. Then he said, 'All that's in the past. I'm happy you're here. I'm happy you came. I always thought of you. Both of you. I swear!'

She turned to look at him. He was bent over, as if he was trying to hide from himself. Somewhere deep within her, a light began to shine. It was dim, but it was there. She stood up, 'I've got to make a call.' She went to her room and locked herself in.

She picked up her mobile phone and punched in Obi's number. She needed to talk to someone. She needed to tell him what she had decided to do.

'Obi!' she cried.

'Mma! Are you all right? What's wrong?'

'Yes, yes, I am fine,' she said impatiently. 'Everything is fine.'

'Has anything happened?' he asked. 'I worried so much when I didn't hear from you and then I heard on the news today about the riots.'

'Yes,' she said. 'The riots. But that's not why I am calling. I am coming home as soon as all this is settled. I've decided to build my mother's house.'

'What?'

260

'And, Obi?'

'Yes? What's brought this on?' He sounded so far away.

'I am my mother's daughter, Obi. I killed her, Obi. I wanted her dead.'

'You are not making sense. Slowly. Start again.'

'I never understood her. I am so sorry.' She was sobbing now. 'I didn't even go to see her in hospital when she was sick. And she asked for me! She asked for me!'

'Listen, when you come home we can talk about this, OK? Something's obviously upset you. I wanted to talk to you anyway. I was thinking, as soon as you get back, we should set the ball rolling. I'll take you to meet my parents.'

'Obi! I didn't even go to see her. Did you hear me?'

'Yes, Yes. And I've just asked you to marry me. Will you marry me? I want you to meet my parents.'

'They have to know whose daughter I am.'

'Of course. They will have to meet your father, too. I know that!'

'They have to know about my mother too, Obi.'

'What? Are you there? The connection is bad.'

'You take me as I am or you don't take me at all.'

'Mma?' His voice flowed down the telephone line and boomed in her ears. 'Mma? Are you all right?' The line crackled. It sounded as if someone was eating mouthfuls of popcorn close to her ears. She hung up and heaved a long sigh. She thought of the future. She did not know if Obi would be there with her, but she hoped he would. One thing she was certain of was that it was time for her to start repaying her mother. She would match her, sacrifice for sacrifice. Blood for blood. B was for blood. Thicker than water. She would go back to Enugu and start on her mother's house. Her spirit would rest in peace. Her ghost could dance-dance in her red shoes.

Outside her door, she could hear her father calling her name.

Notes

The Miss World riots in Nigeria, provoked by a newspaper article by journalist Isioma Daniel, took place in November 2002. To suit events in *Night Dancer*, I have moved it forward to January 2002. Everything else about those riots is true.

A glossary of the Igbo words can be found on my website: www.chikaunigwe.com

Acknowledgements

I am grateful to: the VFL (Flemish Funds for Literature), UNESCO and the Civitella Ranieri centre, the Rockefeller Foundation and the Bellagio Center, H.A.L.D. Denmark, for various grants and fellowships while I was writing this novel; Harold Polis and David Godwin for their professional guidance; Tom Avery and Alex Bowler for being the best editors any writer could ask for; Hans Schippers, my brother, for all his help; Tolu Ogunlesi, Uche Umezurike and Brian Chikwava for reading earlier drafts; Daragh Reeves for being so excited about my writing; Lukas Roegler for being a friend; Jose Branders and René Vandenhoudt, my parents-in-law; Maggie Wilkinson, aka the W . . .; Uju Oranugo; Els Baeten for the babysitting; Ekanem Nkechi Akwaugo Okeke for letting me get away with being a lousy godmother; my parents; my siblings; my Jan and our boys for their support.